BLOOD FOLLOWS
JANE AUSTEN

Judith Cranswick

Acknowledgements

My special thanks to Clio O'Sullivan at Chawton House
Library for all her help during lockdown.
As always thanks to my wonderful beta readers and all who
have helped me. The list is too long to name individually but
be assured I value each and every one of you.

www.judithcranswick.co.uk

Fiction by Judith Cranswick

THE FIONA MASON MYSTERIES
BLOOD ON THE BULB FIELDS
BLOOD IN THE WINE
BLOOD AND CHOCOLATE
BLOOD HITS THE WALL
BLOOD ACROSS THE DIVIDE
BLOOD FLOWS SOUTH
BLOOD FOLLOWS JANE AUSTEN

THE AUNT JESSICA MYSTERIES
MURDER IN MOROCCO
UNDERCOVER GEISHA

STAND ALONE PSYCHOLOGICAL SUSPENSE
ALL IN THE MIND
WATCHER IN THE SHADOWS
A DEATH TOO FAR

SHORT STORY COLLECTIONS
ALL SORTS VOLUME 1
ALL SORTS VOLUME 2
ALL SORTS VOLUME 3

Prologue

Everything had been carefully orchestrated even down to the massed crowds waiting in Freedom Square. Loyal to the regime, every one. The annual parade to mark the Independence Day celebrations was about to begin.

Excitement grew as the distant boom of drums announced the marchpast was fast approaching the square. The doors on the balcony of the impressive neo-classical palace opened and President Barbier, accompanied by his wife, stepped out to the roar of the cheering crowd. He acknowledged his supporters with a dignified wave then walked forward ready to take the salute.

The drum major with his ceremonial mace led the band of the Presidential Guard, resplendent in their red uniforms adorned with more gold trim than the British Household Cavalry, into the square.

The sound of the shot could barely be heard above the noise of the band and the madly cheering crowds. Only as the red stain on Antoine Barbier's white military-style jacket began to grow was it apparent that the president had been hit. For a brief second, his face registered surprise before he clutched his chest with his left hand and slumped forward, grasping onto the marble rail with the other hand.

In the Footsteps of Jane Austen

Welcome to the world of one of Britain's favourite authors, Jane Austen. This popular Footsteps tour will take you to the homes in which she lived during her short life and to the places she visited which helped to inspire the settings for her novels. You will also visit some of the stately homes that have been used as locations for recent film and television versions of her books.

Expert local guides will accompany each visit to ensure you get the most from the experience. You will be able to immerse yourself in Jane's world as you enjoy a Jane Austen Festival event and attend a special Regency ball.

Your tour manager has long been a Jane Austen devotee and in addition to providing entertaining and informative evening talks on Jane's life and work, will be on hand to answer all your questions and ensure your holiday is one you will never forget.

Super Sun Executive Travel
Specialists in Luxury Short Breaks and
Continental Tours

Passenger list

(with Fiona's added comments)

Tour Manager: **Mrs Fiona Mason**
Driver: **Mr Winston Taylor**
Accompanying guest expert: **Miss Madison Clark**

Mr **Franklin Austin** - *Canadian, pleasant, outgoing*
Mrs **Renée Austin** – *French accent*
Mr **Piers Carnegie** – 30s, long hair, Jane enthusiast
Miss **Imogene Carnegie** – long full skirts, stick-thin, intense
Mrs **Estelle du Plessis** – *imposing African, aloof, difficult*
Miss **Ruth Lloyd*** – *timid, self-effacing*
Mrs **Erma Mahoney*** – *Ruth's friend, can be judgemental*
Mr **Michael Selassie** – *Estelle's secretary, bodyguard?*
Mr **Lester Summerhayes*** – *keen photographer*
Mrs **June Summerhayes*** – *astute observer*
Mr **Anthony Trueman*** – *tall stooped, hearing aid*
Mrs **Kathleen Trueman*** – *club organiser, efficient, sociable*

* Book club members

Day One

Our base for the first three nights is The Grand Regency Hotel, Winchester. We can choose to make our own way there or join the feeder coach from London.

At the introductory meeting at six-thirty pm, we will be able to get to know our fellow travellers and meet our tour manager who will outline our programme and answer any questions we may have.

After dinner, there will be a short talk about Jane Austen to tell us a little about her life and family and her road to becoming one of the world's most beloved novelists.

Super Sun Executive Travel

Chapter 1

Fiona picked up the room key card, pulled up the handle on her suitcase and turned towards the lifts. Before she had gone more than a couple of paces, a smiling young woman with long fair hair suddenly jumped in front of her.

'Hello. I see you have a Super Sun label on your case. I presume you're here for the Jane Austen Tour.'

Fiona gave a polite smile, but before she could reply, the girl thrust out a hand and continued, 'I'm Madison Clark. I'm going to be looking after you for the week.'

Fiona felt her eyebrows shoot up to her hairline. 'I beg your pardon!'

The girl chuckled. Her cheeks creased in attractive dimples. 'Yes, I know it says in your literature that your tour manager is a man, but he couldn't make it and there's been a last-minute change of plan. But not to worry, I'm here to make sure everything runs smoothly.'

Fiona held up a hand to halt the girl's bubbling chatter. 'Let me stop you there, Madison.' She took a deep breath. No point in taking out her mounting frustration on the girl. 'It's true that Tom Edwards was involved in an accident last Tuesday, but you are not his replacement. I presume you are the University student accompanying the tour.'

Fiona juggled her bag and room key card to her left hand and shook the hand the girl was still holding out. 'I'm Fiona Mason. The new tour manager.'

Madison glared at her indignantly. 'But Dr Roberts said…' Her jaw tightened. 'I've put a lot of work into this. I've prepared a whole series of lectures. I was planning to do one after dinner tonight.'

'Excellent. I'm sure everyone will look forward to hearing them.' Fiona did her best to swallow her annoyance and sound positive. 'Look, why don't we meet up in the hotel coffee shop and we can sort out exactly what you will be doing. Bring all your material with you and we can work out a programme? It will also give us a chance to get to know each other a little better before everyone else arrives. Give me half an hour just to sort myself out.'

Fiona lifted her case onto the end of the bed, slumped down beside it, rubbing her temples with her fingertips. Could the day get any worse? She'd spent the whole journey feeling utterly wretched and it was all her fault. She should never have let David Rushworth talk her into changing her plans at the last minute. Not that it was fair to blame him. Had she let herself be persuaded too readily as Peter had implied? Probably. Had she seized the chance to put off taking the next step in her relationship too readily? This time, she could well have pushed Peter too far. Was there any going back?

Well she was certainly paying for it now. What a start to the tour! Her boss may have thought he was making life easier for her by finding a Jane Austen 'expert' to help out, but the last thing she needed was a resentful student tagging along no matter how knowledgeable about Jane Austen this Madison might be.

With a weary sigh, she stood up, unzipped the case, took out her uniform and lay it ready to welcome the clients arriving by coach from London at four o'clock. On second thoughts, she'd change into it straight away. It would help assert her authority and it wouldn't do any harm for Madison to see that the role of a tour manager was far more than smiling at the clients.

Her mobile rang as she was hanging up the rest of her clothes.

'Martin!'

'Hi Mum, got your message. Sorry I was out when you phoned earlier. How goes it? There was an awful lot of background noise. It sounded like you were outside somewhere.'

'Actually, I was on the train, though right now I'm in Winchester.'

'Winchester! I thought you said you were planning a trip to London with a friend for the weekend and wouldn't be phoning until you got back in the evening. That's why I rang straight away. Nothing wrong is there?'

'Not at all. I'm working.'

'You said you had no more tours booked until the Christmas markets now the summer season's over.'

'I didn't, but my boss rang on Wednesday to say there was an emergency. I did try and get out of it, but there was no one else and the tour was going to have to be cancelled.'

'Humph. He knows you're a push over.'

She laughed. 'You sound just like your brother. The boss may well have been exaggerating but he has been very good to me. Part timers aren't usually allowed to pick and choose their tours like he lets me do, and he's prepared to manipulate the rotas so that I can work with Winston. Anyone less tolerant would have dropped me a long time ago. On the plus side, according to the weather forecast, this glorious spell of good weather is set to last for the rest of the week.'

'But in the meantime, you have to upset all your plans. So, what exactly are you doing in Winchester? I didn't realise Super Sun did coach tours in the UK. I thought they were all on the continent.'

'This is one of the company's specialist tours celebrating writers like Shakespeare, Dickens and the Bronte sisters. This one's called 'In the Footsteps of Jane Austen.' It's only five days and with only a dozen clients, a local guide booked for every visit and no long-distance travel, it should prove an easy assignment. I did point out that Footsteps tours are advertised as being led by a specialist and I know very little about Jane Austen, so the Tours Manager has arranged for a university student specialising in nineteenth century romantic literature to accompany the tour.'

'Sounds like it'll be a doddle.'

'I hope so.' If only she had the same confidence. 'Actually, darling, I've arranged to meet up with her in about ten minutes, so I need to get a move on. All's well with you I take it. What have you been up to?'

'Nothing special. Just the usual routine. Speak to you next Sunday then. Enjoy your trip.'

'Thank you, darling. You take care. Love you. Bye.'

Madison was already in the café when Fiona arrived. She was sitting at one of the tables by the wall with her back to the entrance, but Fiona could see her reflection in the large wall mirror. Madison was busy talking on her mobile, her expression tight-lipped, two red spots on her dimpled cheeks. Fiona slowed her approach, wondering whether to wait until the girl's call was finished. Suddenly the phone was banged down on the table and Madison rocked back in the chair so violently the front legs lifted off the floor.

Fiona took a step backwards. Should she make a tactful exit and come back in a few minutes when the girl had calmed down? Before she had a chance to move, their eyes met in the mirror. Madison spun round getting to her feet.

'Sorry to startle you like that.' A grudging apology at best.

Fiona shook her head. 'Why don't you sit down while I go and order us some coffees. What would you like?'

'A latte please.'

There was only so long she could take making her order and though Madison's expression was no longer openly hostile, Fiona knew she was going to have to work hard to get the girl on her side.

She sat down facing Madison. 'I've also brought a couple of menus. I missed lunch so I'm going to have a bite to eat. Can I tempt you to anything?'

The only answer she received was a shake of the head.

There was only one other couple in the café, so they didn't have to wait long before the waitress came over with their coffees and took Fiona's order for a toasted tea cake.

'I appreciate all of this is a bit last minute for both of us.'

Fiona slipped a folder from her tote bag. 'I've brought a spare copy of the tour booklet that the clients will have received in case you didn't get one.'

Without a word, Madison pulled the rucksack on the chair next to her onto her lap. She rummaged inside and brought out her copy almost throwing it down onto the table.

'Good.' Fiona gave an encouraging smile. 'You mentioned that you had prepared some talks. You'll have seen in the tour details that Tom Edwards was down to give a talk after dinner this evening, but if you feel...'

'I've got them all here.' Madison dived back into the rucksack and lifted out her laptop. 'My tutor Dr Roberts suggested I started with a biography of Jane's life. We talked about a PowerPoint presentation at the end showing some of the films and television dramas based on the novels showing the stately homes used as film sets. He's lent me the department's digital projector and a screen.'

'That sounds excellent. Do you have a copy of the presentation there?' Fiona moved to the chair alongside Madison so she could see the screen.

It took a few minutes to bring it up.

'I love the way you've interspersed stills from the films with pictures of the actual rooms and gardens as we see them today. It's really impressive. You've done an excellent job.'

When she smiled, the girl was exceptionally pretty. 'I've put a lot of work into it.'

'I can see that. The clients are going to love it.'

'I wanted to put the other talks onto PowerPoint too, but I didn't have time. I made a start, but I didn't get far. It takes forever finding suitable pictures and it was difficult to find anything appropriate for the last one.'

'Not to worry. Do you have your notes with you?'

'They're here.'

Madison clicked onto a word document. There seemed to be a great many closely typed pages.

'Umm. Do you know how long it's going to take?'

'I haven't actually timed it, but about an hour I should think.'

Fiona clicked through the first few pages. It was laid out under side headings – Family, Early Childhood, Romance and so on.

'It's all excellent material, but I wonder if it's perhaps a touch too long. Remember, everyone will have been travelling for much of the day and will probably be quite tired. Perhaps you could just mention that two of her brothers were in the navy without going into detail about their careers and you could leave out some of the sections like this one on family friends. If you aim to talk for thirty to forty minutes, it will leave plenty of time for questions.'

Madison's jaw tightened. Any rapport Fiona had built up was quickly fading away.

'That's when you can use all that extra information. You have to remember, some of your audience will know very little about Jane Austen. They may never have read any of her books and only seen a couple of films of the novels. One or two may be ardent Austen fans and want to chat privately about all the things you've researched but hadn't time for in your talk. I doubt any of that material will be wasted.' Fiona smiled encouragingly.

Madison slammed down the lid of her laptop. 'Then I suppose I better go and rewrite it.'

She got to her feet, tucked her laptop under one arm, hitched the strap of her rucksack over her shoulder and strode to the door.

Fiona let out a long sigh. So much for sorting out a programme for the rest of the talks, but there was no point in calling the girl back. Though she'd only seen the title, when Madison had clicked onto her Jane Austen Talks folder, Fiona had noticed a file labelled 'Feminism and Jane Austen'. It sounded more like one of her university essays. Hardly suitable for this tour, but right now Fiona couldn't face another battle.

'Just take it a day at a time,' she said softly to herself. That had always been one of Bill's maxims. Thoughts of her deceased husband always calmed her nerves.

Chapter 2

The last of the coach party made their way up to their room, leaving Fiona free to speak to Winston. She crossed the lobby to the main doors and hurried down the steps to the coach. The big West Indian driver was locking the luggage compartments but looked up when she called his name. His broad smile lit up his face and he opened his arms wide. She was enveloped in a bear hug, her face buried in his chest. The top of her head reached well below his chin and she had to take a step back to look up at him.

'How is you, sweetheart? I didn't expect to see you 'til November.'

'No this is all a bit last minute. David Rushworth phoned to ask me a few days ago, and I explained I couldn't do it because I was going to London for the weekend to visit a friend. A couple of hours later, he rang back to say he'd tried everyone else and no one was free and could I possibly consider postponing my visit for another time.'

'September is always our busiest month.'

Fiona sighed. 'You know how persistent he can be. Anyway, you don't know how pleased I am to see you. I thought you were booked for the Paris and Loire tour leaving tomorrow.'

'Had a phone call from the boss on Wednesday, didn't I. Said you was doing this trip and had asked for me specially and would I be prepared to do a swap with one of the other drivers.'

Fiona shook her head. 'David Rushworth is such a manipulator. I didn't say that at all. I told him it wasn't convenient as we'd booked tickets for a concert on the Saturday evening besides which I only ever do tours with you as my driver. I thought that would clinch it but that afternoon he got back to me a third time saying he'd managed to swap drivers so you could do the tour. He pointed out, that if I was prepared to cut my weekend a little short, I'd still be able to see the concert on Saturday evening and travel up after lunch the next day with you from Victoria Coach Station. After all the trouble he'd gone to, I could hardly refuse.'

Winston wagged a finger at her. 'You just don't know how to say no, sweetheart. You's got to learn to put your foot down right at the beginning and not let him sweettalk you into things. Still, on the plus side, you did get to the concert.'

Fiona gave a long sigh and shook her head. 'By Thursday evening, I realised I was going to need more time to prepare so I had to cancel the weekend altogether.'

Winston's eyebrows shot up. 'Bet that didn't go down well with your fella.'

'You could say that.' Unbidden, tears welled up behind her eyelids.

An arm wrapped round her shoulders and a large, folded handkerchief appeared in front of her face. She scrubbed her eyes with the back of her hand.

'You two have a row?'

She shook her head. 'Worse than that. I'd have preferred it if he'd shouted at me. All he'd said was that he'd wondered what excuse I'd find this time. I felt so guilty!'

'Perhaps he had a point.'

She stared up at him. In all the time she'd known him and despite all the mistakes she'd made in the job, this was the first time she could remember the supportive Winston ever taking someone else's side against her.

'Do you think I don't know that?' she whispered.

'You gotta make a decision, sweetheart. You can't keep stringing the poor chap along. Either you try and make the relationship work, or you finish it altogether for both your sakes.'

She looked up at him. 'I spent the whole of the train

journey up here telling myself just that. But it's such a massive step and I'm not sure I'm ready for it. I was married to Bill for thirty-four years.'

'But he died well over two years ago now. Your boys have got their own lives and you only see them once in a blue moon. There's nothing to stop you movin' on. You can't spend the next thirty odd years on your own. Even a blind man can see the two of yous is head-over-heels about each other. I can't see the problem.'

'It's so long since I've been on a date, I'm not sure how to handle it. And a whole weekend, just the two of us. It's unnerving. We've had the odd meal alone, but mostly we've been thrown together because of our jobs.'

'You won't know till you try.'

'Bill is the only man I've ever been with. I led a very sheltered existence. I was an only child, and my parents were in their forties when I was born. By the time I was a teenager, when all my schoolfriends were out dancing and going to clubs and whatnot, I was helping Mum. By then, my father was virtually bedridden, and she was his carer. She found it difficult to cope both physically and mentally.'

'That must've been hard for you.'

'Not really. I just accepted it. I suppose that's the reason I became a nurse.'

'Now don't tell me all those young doctors didn't start flirting with a pretty young girl like you.'

She grinned up at him. 'Flatterer!'

'I's right though, ain't I?'

'They did and to be honest, all that sudden attention made me uncomfortable. I just wasn't prepared for it. They called me the ice queen and one of the other nurses told me several of them had placed a bet on which of them could get me into bed first. If it hadn't been for my boss, the consultant anaesthetist, I'd have handed in my notice. He took me under his wing and all the silliness stopped.'

'That was your Bill, was it?'

She nodded. 'As the months went on, working alongside

him as his scrub nurse, I suppose we just got close. Of course, Bill was a lot older than me, but it didn't seem to matter.' She shook her head. 'I'm sorry, Winston. I don't know why on earth I'm telling you all this.'

He patted her hand. 'No worries, sweetheart. I's always here when you wanna talk. Talking helps puts things in perspective. Sorts out what really matters.'

She reached up and kissed him on the cheek.

'And it has, Winston. Thank you for putting up with me.'

~

Peter Montgomery-Jones had almost completed the Times crossword when the telephone rang.

'Sorry to disturb you at home, sir, but I thought you'd like to know…'

'Just a moment. Let me turn down the music.'

Montgomery-Jones picked up the controls of his top-of-the-range sound system and the thunderous section of Wagner's Meistersinger overture was suddenly muted to a murmur.

'My apologies, James. I was having difficulty hearing you. Do go on.'

'No problem, sir. I just wanted to let you know the stranded trade delegation members have arrived from Kinyande. They landed at Brize Norton half an hour ago and are on their way to Marlborough for a debrief.'

'That is good news.'

'Yes and no. One is still missing. He failed to turn up at the airport. They delayed the flight for half an hour, but he didn't appear.'

'They have no idea where he might be?'

'Apparently not.'

'Is there any cause for concern?'

'Possibly not. Right now, we don't have all the details, but there was no message from him, and he failed to answer any of their calls.'

'I see. In all probability, there will turn out to be some simple explanation like forgetting to charge his mobile, but you were right to let me know. I think it best we keep an eye on the situation for now and see what transpires.'

'Certainly, sir.'

~

Anthony and Kathleen Trueman were the first to arrive for the meet-and-greet before dinner. They had introduced themselves when they had arrived with the rest of the book club members on the coach from London. Anthony was the club president though it had been Kathleen who had done all the organising of the holiday for the club members.

'Can I tempt you to one of these?' Fiona asked as she proffered a plate of nibbles.

Anthony, a tall stooped man with thinning grey hair and wearing a hearing aid, accepted one and promptly looked confused trying to work out how he could take the paper napkin with the vol-au-vent in one hand and a glass of white wine in the other.

His wife took it for him and held his glass while he sorted himself out. It was an almost unconscious gesture on her part. Seeing to his needs was clearly automatic.

She turned to Fiona. 'Not for me thank you. I must say, we are all looking forward to this trip immensely. Last year, the book group did the Dickens Footsteps tour, and it was a great success. Unfortunately, we couldn't raise enough people for an exclusive tour this time. It's disappointing because when it was first proposed everyone was very keen. Ten people signed up straight away, but you know how it is.' She shrugged her shoulders. 'On the plus side, it will be interesting to meet other people interested in Austen.'

'How many do you have in your book club?'

'There's seventeen of us now, though of course not everyone can make the monthly get-together. We meet in our house so there's a limit on how many we can squeeze in, but there's rarely more than a dozen of us.'

Fiona turned her head to glance at the door as another group of people came in.

'Don't let me keep you,' Kathleen said with a smile. 'You need to speak with everyone.'

The new arrivals included two new faces, an arty-looking couple in their thirties. His long bushy fair curls were pulled back in a ponytail from a thin delicate face. The woman was similarly thin and lanky though the full ankle-length skirt and long patchwork jacket effectively disguised her figure. Though he appeared lively and outgoing, she seemed considerably more retiring, the pair looked so alike that it was immediately obvious they must be brother and sister.

Fiona held out her hand. 'I'm Fiona Mason, your tour manager. You must be Imogene and Piers.'

'How clever of you to know our names.' Piers gave her a coquettish smile as he took her hand in a weak handshake.

'Not really. I met most of the others when they arrived on the coach.'

'Did you say you were the tour manager?' Imogene wore a puzzled expression.

'That's right.'

'But when we arrived, we met a young girl who said she was the tour manager.'

'That would be Madison. She will be helping to look after you all and she's the person who can answer all your questions on Jane Austen. Unfortunately, at the very last minute the gentleman who usually leads this particular tour and is an Austen expert, couldn't be with us. I'm afraid I don't have his expert knowledge, which is why Madison has joined us. She's the one who'll be giving you a talk on Jane after dinner.' Imogene frowned but before she could protest, Fiona continued, 'Now do go and get yourself a glass of wine or there's orange juice if you'd prefer.'

She didn't have time for a long dispute. Just as Fiona was beginning to wonder if Madison would put in an appearance, the girl walked through the door. She was wearing a distinctly sulky look, but Fiona had more important things to think about right now. Time to get the meeting started or they'd be late for dinner.

The hotel had hosted Austen Footsteps Tours twice a year for the last three years. The manager had everything well in hand, so Fiona had no worries about needing to check up on the arrangements. He had even organised for the group to be served dinner in the small meeting room where the evening talk was due to take place.

As everyone began to take their places at dinner, one of the waiters approached Fiona.

'Excuse me, madam. Before we begin serving, I understand we have one diabetic, a Mr Franklin and two who have requested vegetarian meals, a Mr and Miss Carnegie. Could you point them out to me, please?'

'Piers and Imogene Carnegie are sitting at the far table, but I am not so sure where Mr Franklin is.' Fiona glanced around. 'I believe he is the gentleman at the table by the window with his back to us, next to the lady in the red blouse. You will have to check.'

As the waiters continued to serve the main course, a strident voice cut across the gentle murmur of conversation.

'I don't want that rubbish! I expressly ordered a diabetic meal.'

Fiona leapt to her feet and hurried across.

'Is there a problem?'

The large, big-boned black woman pushed away the plate in front of her so violently that gravy spilt over the pristine tablecloth.

'I require a diabetic meal.'

'Mrs du Plessis, I can only apologise on behalf of the company that the information was not passed on to the hotel. I am sure this young man,' she turned to the waiter with a smile, 'will remedy the situation for you straight away.'

Fiona returned to her seat. Though no one commented on the woman's unreasonable outburst, she received sympathetic glances from her fellow diners, and it was several minutes before the level of chatter resumed its previous hum.

Whether someone at Head Office had slipped up, something Fiona could not remember ever happening before, or the woman had simply failed to tick the box for the special diabetic option when she'd completed the application form, hardly mattered. A difficult passenger could spoil everyone's enjoyment of the tour.

Estelle du Plessis had booked onto the tour less than a week ago and the other African, Michael Selassie, only three days ago. Fiona had not exchanged more than a few words with either of them. Mrs du Plessis had introduced Michael as her secretary. Tall and broad-shouldered, he was dressed like someone about to attend a business conference rather than a coach tour. Fiona had found Estelle's commanding presence intimidating but she wasn't sure what to make of the solemn-faced, reserved Michael Selassie. Anyone looking less ready to enjoy a pleasant holiday, it would be hard to find.

Chapter 3

After they had all eaten, the plates had been cleared away and coffee had been served, it was
time for Madison's talk.

'We are so grateful to Madison for stepping in at the last minute and I know you are all going to give her a very warm welcome.' Fiona gave the girl a smile of encouragement and made her way to an empty chair.

Madison cut a lonely figure at the front of the room. The arrogance had gone and for the first time she looked apprehensive. She began a little hesitantly, but as she warmed to her subject her voice became stronger and she spent more time looking at her audience than at her notes. Although she had taken Fiona's advice and cut great swathes of detail from her original talk, it still lasted for almost an hour.

No hands went up for questions, but the applause was genuine enough.

'Thank you again, Madison. There is no need to rush away, everyone. Do help yourself to more coffee and if you do think of any questions, Madison will be here so please don't hesitate to ask.'

Fiona turned and patted Madison on the shoulder. 'Well done, you.'

'Any chance of getting a real drink?' Estelle du Plessis's penetrating voice cut across the hum of chatter that had begun.

'That woman hasn't stopped drinking since she got here,' Madison muttered.

Fiona had noticed that Estelle had accepted a glass of wine from a waiter when she had first arrived and downed it in a single swallow before replacing the glass on the waiter's tray and helping herself to another. Later, when they all took their places for dinner, she had sat down with a full glass in her hand. Not the most sensible behaviour if the woman was a diabetic.

One of the book club ladies approached, waiting for them to finish their conversation.

'I think Mrs Summerhayes has a question for you, Madison.'

'Do call me June.' The woman smiled gratefully at Fiona then turned to Madison. 'You mentioned about one of Jane's brothers being adopted.'

'Edward. He was adopted by Thomas Knight. He was a wealthy cousin of Edward's father, but he and his wife had no children…'

This was a good opportunity for Fiona to slip away and check up on Estelle du Plessis. By now, most people had migrated to the long tables at the back of the room where a waitress had just brought in fresh pots of coffee. Nonetheless, it wasn't difficult to spot the imposing figure of Estelle du Plessis. Not only was she tall, she was wearing a vibrantly coloured red and black kaftan with a scarf of the same material wound turban-style around her head.

'Mrs du Plessis, we didn't get a chance to talk earlier, I hope your journey to Winchester wasn't too tiring today. Have you come far?'

'Oh no. We arrived in England two weeks ago.' The smile was quite genuine and there was a shrewd look in the black eyes that missed nothing. She knew exactly why Fiona had sought her out. The woman may have had several glasses of wine, but she was far from drunk.

Michael Selassie suddenly appeared at Estelle's elbow holding out a cup of coffee.

'Thank you, Michael. Fetch one for Fiona, would you?'

He gave Fiona a brief nod and turned back to the table before Fiona had a chance to say she didn't want another.

'How long are you staying over in England?'

'That remains to be seen. Perhaps indefinitely. I haven't made up my mind.'

'What was it about this tour that attracted you?'

Estelle chuckled and her plump cheeks wobbled. 'When I saw it was focused on Jane Austen, it brought back memories of my governess. She was English. My father insisted that all his children should learn to speak English fluently at an early age. Miss Pettigrew adored Jane Austen and read all her novels to me. The woman was a confirmed romantic. She loved the Bronte sisters as well, but Austen was her passion. I spent many happy hours listening to those stories.'

'Then I hope this holiday will bring back those pleasant memories.'

At least the woman appeared to have calmed down. Perhaps things would not turn out as problematic as Fiona had feared.

For the next half hour everyone mingled, and then one or two people began making tracks for bed.

Fiona was talking with a group of book club members when she became aware of a commotion behind her at the far side of the room.

'You're drunk.' Madison's shrill voice caused every head to turn.

'And you, young lady, are extremely rude.' Though the voice was low, every word could be heard in the embarrassed silence that had descended on the room.

Fiona had rarely moved more quickly. 'Apologise now.'

Madison's bottom lip trembled. 'Well, she is,' she mumbled, her voice barely audible.

'Now!'

'Sorry.' Madison didn't even look at Estelle before rushing from the room.

Fiona turned to Estelle du Plessis. 'Please accept my apology.'

Michael appeared at Estelle's shoulder and deftly removed what looked like a whiskey glass from Estelle's hand.

'I'll see she gets to her room.' With that, he steered Estelle towards the door.

'My bag. Fetch my bag.' Estelle stopped abruptly.

'Where did you leave it?'

'Over on my chair.' She pointed to the seat on the front row where she'd been sitting for the talk.

Michael took only a few long-legged strides to reach the spot.

'It is not here.'

'For goodness' sake.'

Estelle joined him and they both searched under the chairs.

'Someone has stolen it.' Estelle's voice boomed across the room.

The half-dozen people still remaining hurriedly joined in the search.

'Is this it?' Imogene picked up a voluminous black velvet pouch embroidered in gold with a long gold chain strap.

'Give it to me.'

Estelle strode towards her, almost snatched the bag from the younger woman's hands and swept out of the door.

Michael hurried after her pausing only to give a brief nod of thanks to Imogene.

'Well really,' muttered Imogene and turned to her brother. 'She could at least have said thank you.'

A stunned silence followed. Everyone decided to call it a night, embarrassed at having been made to witness such a scene. Within five minutes the room was empty, and Fiona was free to make her own way upstairs.

She stood at the door of Madison's room her hand ready to knock when she heard voices from inside. Or rather Madison's voice. She couldn't make out the words but the was no mistaking the anger. Every now and again the torrent of invective would stop, only to start up again thirty seconds later. Presumably the girl was on the phone. Suddenly the volume increased.

'Mean, vindictive bitch! It's all her fault.'

It sounded as though Madison was right behind the door. Just as quickly the voice faded. The girl must be pacing up and down the room.

It was clear that any attempt to talk with Madison right now would only exacerbate the situation. Best to let her cool down and speak to her first thing in the morning.

Although it was only a few minutes after ten o'clock by the time Fiona crawled into bed, it felt like an incredibly long day. Not that it was over yet. She still had one more phone call to make and she wasn't sure what sort of reception she would get. Nonetheless, she had important bridges to build.

'I know I said I'd phone when I got to the hotel, but it's been full on ever since I arrived.'

'I thought the reason you decided to travel up independently was in order to have a couple of hours to settle in and check on all the arrangements before the coach arrived.'

'It didn't quite work out like that. The young student who is acting as a guest Austen expert was already here and we had a lot to discuss.' No need to go in to detail. 'Besides not everyone joined the coach. One couple live on the outskirts of Bristol so no point in catching a feeder coach all the way to London only to have to retrace the journey back to Winchester. Especially when we finish the tour in Bath which is no more than half an hour from their home.'

'I see.'

'How was the concert last night?' she asked as brightly as she could manage.

'Excellent.'

'I'm sorry I missed it.'

When he didn't reply, she continued. 'I can't apologise enough for messing you about over accepting this job, Peter. I'm genuinely sorry. At first, I thought I'd be able to do as David Rushworth suggested – spend most of the weekend with you, picking up the coach at Victoria after lunch. But as I explained after the phone call with Tom Edwards, the usual

Jane Austen Footsteps guide, and seeing all the stuff he emailed me, I realised just how much more time I needed to get my head round it all.' It sounded a pathetic excuse even to her own ears.

'If you say so.'

'Please Peter, don't make me feel any worse. Not after the day I've had.'

'Bad journey?'

'The journey itself was fine. Just one change at Woking, but I didn't have long to wait for the train. But things have been going downhill ever since I got to the hotel.'

Peter chuckled. 'Please tell me you are not going to end up with another dead body on this tour.'

'Do not jest, Peter. The way things are going, not only will there be a dead body, I'm the one who will be charged as the murderer!'

Now he was doing nothing to hide his laughter. 'You assured me that this trip was going to be the easiest one yet, with no research needed and all the arrangements made. You said it would be a relaxing holiday as far as you were concerned.'

'No. I said that is what Mr Rushworth told me when he talked me into doing it. I should have known by now that's what Super Sun's Tours Director always tells me.'

Fiona spent the next ten minutes recounting what had happened. When the call ended, she put out the light and settled down to sleep.

Even though it had been an exhausting day, she tossed and turned for some time, but it wasn't Madison Clark or the overbearing Estelle du Plessis who occupied her thoughts.

Hand on heart, her cancelling the plans to spend the weekend in Peter's flat in London was probably less to do with her line manager's persuading plea than her own lack of courage to take the next step in her relationship with Peter. Much as she was attracted to the handsome, charming MI6 director, theirs was something of a tempestuous liaison. Her marriage to Bill had always been on an even keel. They had always been more best friends than passionate lovers and not just because Bill was so much older. She could not remember a single time when he had lost his temper with her. Though to do him justice, neither had Peter. She was always the one to go off the deep end. Naturally there were times when she and Bill had disagreed, but he had never driven her to such lengths. Even now she missed Bill, his calming influence, his quiet understanding. When he died, it never occurred to her that she would ever lose her heart to another man.

The problem was that no matter how much she argued with herself that she and Peter had no future for all sorts of reasons, all that rationale went straight out of the window the moment she saw him. But was that magnetic attraction enough to sustain a lasting relationship?

She propped herself up on one elbow and punched her pillow before settling herself down. Think about something else, she told herself firmly.

Day Two

This morning we take a short drive to the village of Steventon where Jane Austen was born in the rectory in December 1775. She was the seventh of eight children born to the Revd George Austen and his wife Cassandra. It was here that she wrote her first three novels, Pride and Prejudice, Northanger Abbey, and Sense and Sensibility. Although the rectory was pulled down in 1824, St Nicholas Church, where her father, eldest brother and nephew were rectors for over 100 years, is still standing. We will be met by the village archivist who will explain the church's memorials and show us the churchyard where Jane's eldest brother and his family are buried.

From Steventon, we will travel the short distance to Chawton Cottage, Jane's final home. After the death of her father, Jane's mother was left in difficult circumstances and for the next four years, she and her two unmarried daughters moved several times before settling in Southampton in 1806. In 1809, Jane's brother Edward who had been adopted by her father's well-to-do cousin, provided his mother and sisters with a small cottage rent-free on his estate at Chawton.

This humble eighteenth century redbrick cottage was the happy home in which Jane redrafted her first three novels and where she wrote Mansfield Park, Emma and Persuasion.

After the death of Jane's sister, Cassandra in 1845, the cottage passed through many hands until it was bought by the Jane Austen Society and was opened to the public in 1949 as the Jane Austen's House Museum. It was granted Grade 1 listed status in 1963.

When we arrive, a museum guide will tell us more about Jane's life in the cottage before we each make our own way to look at the rooms and the various exhibits including her writing desk, letters written by Jane and personal effects belonging to her and her family. We will then be free to explore the gardens that she and her sister Cassandra so lovingly tended.

After lunch in a local public house our final visit of the day will be to Chawton House Library for a guided tour. The house was built by the Knight family in the 1580s on the site of an earlier medieval building and became the home of Jane's brother Edward Knight.

The house was taken over by American entrepreneur and philanthropist Sandy Lerner in 1993 with the aim of restoring the building as an important literary heritage of women writers. In 2003, its magnificent collection of over 9,000 books and manuscripts was made available to scholars in partnership with the University of Southampton. The house has been open to the public since 2015.

Super Sun Executive Travel

Chapter 4

Fiona took her time getting ready the next morning. Her first task of the day would not be a pleasant one. Though she had decided that nothing would be gained by talking with Madison last night, it didn't mean that she could let the girl get away with such behaviour.

Madison's room was only a few doors down the corridor from her own. At first there was no response to her knock, and she wondered if the girl had already gone down to breakfast. She knocked again calling out her name.

The door opened just enough for a face to peer out.

'Are you going to let me in?'

It took a moment or two before Madison pulled open the door fully and marched back inside. She perched on the edge of the bed staring up at Fiona, a defiant expression on her face.

'That woman started it. She called me ignorant. How was I to know her name was pronounced Duplessy?'

'That really isn't the point, is it?' Fiona sat down beside her and continued calmly. 'You are here in an official capacity. However difficult some clients can be, it's your job to be polite at all times and never ever lose your temper. You know that as well as I do.'

'Are you going to send me home? If Dr Roberts finds out it could affect my future grades.'

'Before anything else is decided, you are going to make a full apology to Mrs du Plessis.'

Madison hung her head, clenching and unclenching her fists in her lap.

Fiona stood up. 'She may already be down at breakfast.' Madison appeared reluctant to get to her feet. 'The longer you put it off the more difficult it's going to be.'

Breakfast was in the main dining room. Most of the Super Sun party were sitting in a section alongside one of the large picture windows looking out over a small garden area, but Estelle du Plessis was not one of them. Fiona looked around the rest of the L-shaped room.

'Wait here a moment,' she said to Madison. 'I'll see if she's sitting round the corner.'

The tables were filling up fast and Fiona walked slowly looking along each row to check that she had not missed her. On her way back, she spotted Michael at the buffet table.

'Good morning, Mr Selassie. Have you seen Mrs du Plessis this morning?'

He turned to face her, bowing his head slightly as he said, 'Good morning to you, Fiona. Madam du Plessis has decided to have a light breakfast in her room today.' Unlike Estelle who spoke English fluently and had no discernible accent, it was evident that Michael was less familiar with the language. Though he appeared to have no difficulty understanding English, it took him much longer to frame a reply. Perhaps that explained his reticence to join in the social chitchat.

'But she will be joining us on the tour this morning?'

'Most certainly. We will both be down in the hotel lobby at nine o'clock as requested.'

He gave another brief bow and returned to helping himself to breakfast.

Michael was certainly not a man for small talk. Not once had she seen the man smile. His face was devoid of emotion. It was difficult to know what to make of him. With his shaved head and hairless chin, it was difficult even to assess his age, though standing next to him she realised he was perhaps a good deal older than she had first assumed.

Madison was still hovering just inside the door. Fiona went to join her. 'Mrs du Plessis is having room service this morning. I'm not sure that this would be the best time for you to disturb her. Several of our other guests are here. Perhaps you might like to go and join them and make them feel welcome.'

Fiona watched her slouch away. She was tempted to call after her and tell her to put a smile on her face. This was not a good way to start the day. Taking a couple of deep breaths to calm herself, she decided that she should follow her own advice and do the same.

'May I join you?'

'Please do.' Renée moved her handbag from the chair next to her, there was a definite French lilt to her accent.

She and her husband Franklin were the Canadian couple who had travelled up from London with the book group.

'My daughter-in-law is Canadian. My son's been working over in Montreal for what must be eight years now,' Fiona said.

'We live in the centre, in Winnipeg which is where I was born and raised. I worked in Quebec for four years which is where I met my lovely wife here.' Franklin leant over and put an arm around Renée's shoulders, giving her a quick hug.

'That explains your lovely accent.' Fiona smiled at Renée.

'Not really. I'm not a Quebec native. I was actually born in Africa. My father was in the French diplomatic service. We stayed on after independence for another ten years but when the military junta took over, my parents emigrated to Canada and I went with them.'

Something in the woman's voice prompted Fiona to say, 'That must have been a difficult time.'

'It was. My brother and my newly married older sister stayed behind. I was very close to my sister.' Fiona noticed a sadness in the woman's voice.

'Have the two of you lost touch?'

Renée picked a sachet of sweetener from the sugar pot and took her time slowly stirring it into her coffee before she answered. 'She died.'

Time to change the subject. 'So are the two of you over here on holiday?'

'That's right. We came over three weeks ago, and it's been nonstop ever since. We wanted to see as much as

31

possible. All pretty exhausting so we decided we'd take a bit of a break from the driving…'

'And sorting out hotels every other day,' Renée interrupted with a soft laugh.

'That too. Which is why we decided to book a tour and let someone else sort out all the arrangements. These dates fitted in with our plans and we were keen to see Bath.'

'And with our surname being Austin, it sort of clinched it.'

'Do I take it you're not ardent Jane Austen enthusiasts then?'

Franklin gave her a sheepish grin. 'Not specially. We've seen some of the films of course.'

'Not to worry. I must confess I'm no expert myself. Most of what I know of her work is from the TV dramas and films. I'm not sure I've read any of her books since I was at school. That's why the company arranged for Madison to join us.'

'We enjoyed the young lady's talk last night and we learnt a lot. I hadn't realised that it was only Jane's family and close friends who knew she was a writer.'

'And it was a real surprise,' Renée interrupted, 'to hear that not all her books were published in her lifetime.'

'I'm sure Madison will be a great asset.' Fiona mentally crossed her fingers.

She glanced over Franklin's shoulder at Madison who was sitting a couple of tables away. Even though the girl had her back to her, it was clear from her lively body language that she was having an animated conversation with Imogene and Piers. Imogene's eyes widened and she shook her head in disbelief which made Fiona wonder what they could be talking about.

~

There was a knock at the door and James Fitzwilliam entered.

'Your coffee, sir.'

'Thank you, James. Any more information on our missing trade delegate?'

'Not yet, sir. I'll chase it up.'

'Good man.'

Montgomery-Jones continued with the paperwork in front of him, but when he sensed his assistant was still hovering on the far side of his desk, he stopped writing.

'Something on your mind?'

'I was just thinking about the situation in Kinyande. It strikes me as strange that three weeks after his assassination there has still been no official announcement concerning the arrest of Barbier's killer. There's been nothing on the general media either.'

'Your point being?'

'I would have expected at the very least a scapegoat to have been presented to the people on the day of the assassination if only to save face. "Gunman killed as he tried to flee from the scene of the crime", sort of thing.'

'Precisely. And what does that tell you?'

'That the government are floundering. It was several days before they came out with a statement that such an atrocity by the Peoples Party would be met with reprisals, but everything has gone unusually quiet ever since.'

'And neither the Peoples Party nor any of the smaller revolutionary groups have claimed responsibility. Speaking to Jean-Claude Durand this morning, I gained the impression that the French are of the opinion that Barbier may have been killed by one of his inner cabinet.'

'I suppose they are the best placed to know. Kinyande was one of their colonies. Several of our people in the area have the same hunch, but...' Fitzwilliam hesitated.

'You do not agree?'

'I was just a little surprised, that's all. I thought Barbier had surrounded himself with his loyal supporters. Does Durand have anyone in mind?'

'None that he shared with me.'

'I suppose the obvious suspect would be Vannier. He did take over straight away.'

'Maybe, but he was Barbier's deputy and therefore the obvious choice. He also said that it would only be as Acting President until a new leader could be elected.'

'He could be feigning reticence while he builds up support to ensure his election next month.'

'Possibly. The word is that there is so much infighting that no single person is proving a strong enough candidate for the others to rally around. The French are hoping that Barbier's widow will take over the reins. In their opinion, she is the only one the rest of the inner cabinet would be prepared to accept. The problem being that no one has seen Eshe Barbier since the assassination.'

'Could she have been taken out by the rebels or one of the other contenders?'

'Jean-Claude would not commit himself, but he appears to be of the opinion that she is either dead or imprisoned until a rival candidate is firmly in control.'

'Which does not bode well for the stability of the country.'

'As things stand, Kinyande is a powder keg.'

'Which could set light to major conflict in the whole of Central Africa as the adjoining countries side with the different factions.' Montgomery-Jones sighed.

~

Winston answered Fiona's call straight away.

'I'm so sorry I had to cancel our breakfast meeting. I had a problem to sort out.'

'No worries, sweetheart. Everything okay now?'

'We'll have to see. I'll tell you about it later. Anyway, are we still all set for a nine o'clock departure?'

'I'll be there. I've checked online and there's no traffic holdups mentioned so everything should run as smooth as clockwork.'

'Thanks, Winston.'

She rang off, dropped her phone on the bed and went to clean her teeth. At least with Winston as her driver, that was one less thing she had to worry about.

Fiona glanced at her watch. Gone nine o'clock and neither Estelle nor Michael had appeared. The Grand Regency Hotel lay north east of the city centre on a relatively quiet side street. Although there was a small pull-in area immediately outside for drop-off and pickup, the coach could not wait for long.

After five minutes there was still no sign of the missing guests. So much for Michael's assurances. She had stressed at the introductory meeting just how important it was to stick to times especially as the coach was only allowed to stop long enough for drop off and pick up. Reluctant to leave them behind on the first day, she decided to ask one of the receptionists to ring their rooms.

The elegantly uniformed young man behind the desk looked up as she approached, but before she could make her request, his colleague a little further along the line forestalled her.

'Mrs Mason. There was a note left on the desk for you earlier.' She looked under the counter and brought out an envelope and handed it over.

'I wasn't expecting anything.' Fiona stared at her printed name on the front. 'Do you know who left it?'

'I believe it may have been the young man in a baseball cap. He came in with several guests who arrived in a minibus about half an hour ago. I found it on the desk when they left and as he was the only one who didn't check in, I assume it was him.'

'How strange.' Fiona was about to open it when the lift doors opened, and Michael stepped out.

'Was there anything else you wanted, Mrs Mason?'

Fiona turned back to the young man behind the desk. 'Not anymore. Thank you. Thank you both.'

She stuffed the note in her bag and joined Michael.

'Estelle not with you?'

'I apologise on her behalf. As we were waiting for the lift, Madame du Plessis decided that she might need an extra phial of insulin. Ah! Here she is now.'

Estelle, resplendent in kaftan and scarf in various shades of yellow and green in a bold geometric design emerged from the lift and strode towards the assembled group.

'Now we're all here, let's make our way to the coach which is waiting outside.'

As the rest of the party began filing through the revolving doors, Madison went to speak to the formidable Estelle. Fiona stood at the entrance discreetly watching the exchange whilst ostensibly waiting for everyone to make their way outside. She was too far away to hear what was being said and Madison had her back to her so she couldn't see the girl's face. Estelle's expression was as imperious as ever, but to Fiona's relief, she appeared to accept that the girl was sufficiently contrite.

Estelle swept through the doors leaving Fiona and Madison to bring up the rear.

'I grovelled,' Madison said in answer to Fiona's raised eyebrow. 'Her majesty deigned to accept it.'

'Then lesson learnt, I trust.'

There was plenty of room in the coach but nearly everyone had chosen to sit with a partner. Fiona noticed that Estelle had distanced herself from the others with Michael two seats behind her.

Picking up the microphone, Fiona waited until everyone had settled into their seats.

'Good morning everyone. Before we start, I appreciate most of you have already met our driver, when he drove you up from London, but for those of you who joined us at the hotel, let me introduce you to Winston.'

The big West Indian turned and gave a wave. 'Hi there.'

'He's going to be with us throughout the next five days.

We are going to begin today with a visit to Steventon. This small village, as I'm sure you'll all remember from Madison's talk last night, is where Jane was born and spent her childhood years. It's less than twenty miles away so it won't be long before we get there. Now let's get going.'

Chapter 5

The surrounding countryside was looking its best in the autumn sunshine as the church archivist led them across the field to see the pump which was all that was left of the parsonage, Jane's first home. The first visit of the morning passed without incident, although there was little to see except the small church of St Nicholas where Jane's father had been rector.

'Any chance of finding somewhere for a coffee before we get to the Jane Austen House? I looked it up on the Internet and it doesn't seem to have a café,' asked Kathleen as Fiona went to help her up the coach steps.

'Next on the agenda,' Fiona said. 'We'll be stopping in one of the villages on the way at a place which used to be an old coaching inn and posting house back in the eighteenth century. It was on one of the main stagecoach routes and we know Jane was taken to The Wheatsheaf as a child.'

'How lovely.' She turned to her husband. 'Did you hear that, Anthony?'

Fiona smiled. 'Don't worry. I shall be telling everyone, once we're all on board the coach.'

One of the advantages of a late September tour was that the high season crowds no longer thronged the major tourist sites. There was plenty of room in the old inn. Despite the low beamed ceilings, half panelled walls and dark wood furniture, there was little that Jane Austen would recognise.

Fiona collected her coffee and although three or four of her passengers had already taken their seats in the bar, she decided to take her drink through into the garden and enjoy the sunshine. Outside, half a dozen people were sitting at a large picnic table alongside a tall hedge that formed the boundary with the adjacent garden centre.

'Do come and join us, Fiona. You mustn't sit all on your own. We can easily squeeze up a bit,' called out Erma Mahoney, one of the book group.

'If you're sure,' she replied as they all shifted further along the bench to make room.

A few minutes later, Imogene and Piers emerged from inside and made their way to a nearby table. As Imogene lifted her leg to step over the bench, her cup tipped, spilling her coffee.

'Now look what's happened! It's all over my skirt.'

Fiona stood up, ready to go and help, but Piers had things in hand.

'Calm down, Sis. It's only a splash. Most of it ended up in the saucer.'

He took the offending cup from her and carefully laid it on the table then knelt down and proceeded to wipe at the offending mark with a paper napkin. 'There we go. It'll soon dry.'

'But the stain will show.'

'No one will notice. It's only a small patch and that flowery pattern will hide it.'

Imogene continued to stand with her fists clutched to her chest and her eyes still glistening with tears.

Piers got to his feet and put an arm around her shoulder. 'Come on. Let's go and get you another coffee.'

As the couple began to make their way back inside, Estelle's penetrating voice rang out, 'What a fuss over a few spilt drops.'

Imogene stopped mid-stride, but Piers hurried her on.

'That was uncalled for,' Kathleen admonished.

Estelle shrugged her shoulders. 'The woman is clearly unstable.'

An embarrassed silence descended on the group as all but the unrepentant Estelle, buried their noses in their coffee cups.

'It's quite pleasant out here, isn't it? Quite a sun trap,

sheltered from the wind,' Fiona said. As an attempt to change the subject, it was a pretty poor effort, but on the spur of the moment she was forced to fall back on the old British standby for small talk.

'Is this weather typical for England at this time of year?' asked Estelle, seemingly unaware of the cool atmosphere her earlier comment had aroused.

'We do sometimes have a warm sunny spell like this in September, but British weather is never predictable. Is this your first time over here?'

'It is. Both my brothers were sent to boarding school, but I had a governess. My father was a diplomat, so my parents were away a great deal of the time.'

'That must have been a lonely childhood for you,' said Kathleen. Her tone lacked the sympathy that the words might suggest.

Estelle shrugged her large shoulders and gave a rueful smile. 'I suppose so, but I had Miss Pettigrew, my governess. She was very special to me.'

Erma gave a sudden start, attempting to pull the edges of her cardigan loosely draped over her shoulders more tightly around herself. It was a second or two before Fiona realised that she must be sitting on the sleeve.

'I'm so sorry.'

She was at fault, but such a simple mistake surely didn't deserve the momentary venomous look on Erma's face.

'No problem,' Erma muttered dropping her gaze. 'It has got a little chilly hasn't it?'

When it came time to start ushering everyone back onto the coach, Fiona discovered Madison in another animated discussion with Piers and Imogene who had remained inside after Estelle's uncalled-for taunt.

Madison had a decidedly guilty look as she joined Fiona walking back to the coach.

'How was Imogene?' Fiona asked.

'Fine. Why?'

'She spilt her coffee when she was outside and seemed a little upset. She didn't mention it to you?'

Madison shook her head. 'No. Actually, we had a great discussion about Jane's views on attitudes to women in Regency England. Those two really know their stuff.'

Fiona smiled. Madison was not the most sensitive to other people's moods. At least she could be thankful that the girl had lost the sullen, resentful attitude of earlier. To give Madison her due, she had been trying very hard since breakfast. Having overstepped the mark with Estelle du Plessis, she must be concerned that one more step out of line and she'd be sent packing.

'Welcome to the Jane Austen House Museum. This little cottage is much too small for me to be able to show you all round as a group, but I would like to explain a few things before you make your own way round the house. It's a lovely day so if you would all like to follow me, let's move into the garden where you can all sit down and be more comfortable.'

The woman who welcomed them at Jane's last home was a pleasant, round-faced middle-aged woman with a pleasing voice. Outside on the grass there was a long table with a bench and a few chairs. There weren't quite enough seats for everyone, and Fiona and Madison joined Michael and Franklin standing behind.

'Have any of you ever visited the homes of any other writers?' the guide began.

'Several of us did a Charles Dickens tour with our book club members last year, and we were taken to his London house in Doughty Street,' said Kathleen.

'Imogene and I went to Greenway, Agatha Christie's house a few years back,' piped up Piers.

'That's an excellent example of a house that remains exactly as the author left it,' said their guide. 'As Jane Austen enthusiasts, I'm sure you are all well aware that Jane was by no means well known in her lifetime. The most popular writer back then was Sir Walter Scott. It's only thanks to the

Jane Austen Society who raised the funds to buy this little cottage that we have this museum today. The Jane Austen Society was founded in 1940 by only a handful of people in nearby Alton. It took a further nine years for them to raise funds and it's thanks to their perseverance that this house was opened to the public in 1949. We have done our best to recreate the cottage as it would have been at the time the Austen women were living here. Since then, we've been lucky enough to acquire many family items in the collection on display. These include the only three pieces of jewellery known to have been owned by Jane, a topaz cross, a turquoise gold ring and a turquoise beaded bracelet. There is also a second topaz cross that belonged to Cassandra. They were given to them by their brother Charles. He was an officer in the Royal Navy and he bought the crosses with prize money he received from the capture of an enemy ship. You can see them upstairs in what is designated our treasures room.'

Their guide went on to point several other noteworthy items to look out for before asking if anyone had any questions.

'I noticed when we got off the coach, there's what looks like a large window at the front of the house that's been bricked up. Was there a reason for that?' asked June Summerhayes.

The guide nodded. 'Well spotted. Before Edward gave the cottage to his mother and sisters, he made several changes to what used to be the estate manager's house. As you will have seen, there is no garden between the old front of the house and the street. Although today, it might seem a relatively quiet country road, back then this was the main thoroughfare from London to Winchester. Anyone passing by on the stagecoach would be able to look straight in, so Edward had the parlour window bricked up to give the family more privacy. As you'll see when you go in, light comes in through the side window facing onto this side garden.' She pointed to the last window at the right side of the building.

There were no more questions, so everyone got ready to move off into the museum.

'You will find information cards in every room. As I mentioned the house is quite small, so I suggest not more than four or five people per room. A few of you might like to start in the outbuildings.'

Fiona and Madison hung back to give the rest of the party first choice.

'I don't think anyone went into the kitchen,' their guide pointed out. 'It's the door just to the left of the entrance.'

'Have you been here before?' asked Madison.

Fiona shook her head.

'I've been a couple of times. Once on a school visit and then more recently as part of my course at uni. Originally this kitchen was detached from the house as was the case with so many old buildings, because of fire risk I suppose. It was incorporated into the main building in the 1700s, though they never knocked through to make an internal door.'

They entered the house straight into the drawing room. Lester and June Summerhayes were just leaving so Fiona and Madison had the room to themselves. There was a narrow vestibule between it and the dining room.

'That window would have been the front door in Jane's time, and this is the famous squeaking door into the dining parlour,' Madison explained.

'Squeaking door?'

'Jane was very secretive about her writing and she refused to let anyone oil the hinges on the door. That way, when she heard it being opened, she had a few seconds to hide her manuscript. I think the thing that I find most fascinating in the whole house is her little writing table. I'll show you.'

Madison's plans were thwarted. A small group were already gathered in the room.

'Shall we go upstairs and come back later?' Fiona suggested.

Madison led the way up the narrow staircase and stopped

on the small landing.

'There are several people in the bedroom at the moment.'

'Not a problem,' said Fiona as she joined her at the window looking out over the back garden. 'I hadn't appreciated just how extensive the garden was. It's beautifully kept.'

'As it would have been when Jane was here. Jane was a keen gardener as was Cassandra and their mother. Over to the right, you'll see the outbuildings – the bake house and the old stables where they kept the pony trap.'

Kathleen and Anthony emerged from the bedroom.

'I'm so sorry, have we been holding you up?'

'Not at all,' Fiona assured her. 'You take as long as you like. There's no rush.'

One of the advantages of letting the rest of her party go ahead, Fiona decided, was that she could take her time. She peered into one of the closets on the left of the fireplace which closed off a blue and white pottery washstand with a mirror in a stand perched behind it. They took their time examining the various upstairs rooms, not that they had the rooms entirely to themselves. They had to linger a little longer in what was known as the Admiral's room where Jane's brother slept when he visited, before they could move next door. It gave Fiona time to read the information boards on Jane's seafaring brothers that covered the whole of one wall.

A door led through to a narrow room where the Austen treasures – Jane's shawl, a patchwork quilt made by the three Austen women as well as the jewellery their guide had described earlier – were displayed behind a glass panel.

'I presume the crosses were intended to be worn as pendants?' Fiona asked.

Madison nodded. 'I presume so. They're quite big, aren't they?'

Madison was in her element. If Fiona had any doubts about sending the girl packing on that first evening, they were fast disappearing. Everyone was allowed one chance.

She herself had made enough blunders in her new job. Having someone with such obvious enthusiasm for her subject, could only be an asset.

~

The meeting had proved every bit as unproductive as he'd anticipated. As Peter Montgomery-Jones walked over the bridge towards Vauxhall Cross, it began to rain. Once inside the modern futuristic MI6 Headquarters, he decided to take the stairs to the top floor. He barely had time to get through the door of the outer office before James Fitzwilliam was on his feet.

'The Foreign Secretary's office has been on the line, sir. They would like you to call the Minister PDQ.'

Montgomery-Jones raised his eyebrows. 'Did they give any indication of what it was about?'

'Not to me, sir. But they did stress that it was urgent.'

'Give me a moment to take off my coat then get me a line.'

'Certainly, sir.'

Montgomery-Jones entered his inner office and hung up his coat with a sigh. This did not bode well. What crisis was about to land on his department?

'Good morning, Minister. You wished to speak to me.'

'Thank you for getting back so promptly. You are aware that one of the men from the trade mission has gone missing somewhere in Kinyande.'

'I was aware, sir.'

'This morning, I had a visit from the Minister of Trade and Industry. Seems the missing man was a personal friend. The Minister is anxious that we take steps to extract him.'

'There is little point in sending in a team if we have no idea where he is.'

'Which is exactly what I told him, but he was quite distraught and insists we take diplomatic steps.'

'Without an embassy in the country, I fail to see how that

can be accomplished.'

'Quite. All I'm asking is that you and your department keep a close watching brief on what is going on in Kinyande and perhaps you can make a few discreet enquiries amongst your foreign counterparts.'

Montgomery-Jones stifled a sigh. 'We are already monitoring the situation, Minister. We will do our utmost, but the chances of success are slim at best.'

'That is all I ask.'

The call ended and he sat back in his chair muttering half under his breath, 'Miracles we can do immediately; the impossible can take a little longer.'

Chapter 6

Everyone was bubbling with excited chatter about their visit as Fiona ushered them across the road. Lunch had been booked in the village pub *The Greyfriar,* which lay opposite the Jane Austen House Museum. The place had an olde-worlde look and feel but the building was probably not around during the period that Jane and her family lived in the village.

Despite the time of year, the weather remained summery and despite the slight breeze, half the party chose to sit in the beer garden at the back of the building.

'I think it's mainly the book club people who have opted to stay inside,' said Madison. 'They do seem to congregate together.'

'With only a dozen passengers, it would be nice if the party didn't divide into factions, but they are the older members of the group and the chairs are more comfortable in here than the picnic table benches. I think it might be a good idea, if we two split up as well. Which would you prefer?'

'I'll stay here, if you like.'

Fiona was a little surprised. She'd expected Madison to opt to join the younger ones, but then perhaps the girl was attempting to maintain as much distance as possible from Estelle du Plessis who had already gone into the garden.

Outside, the rest of the party were sitting at one of the large picnic tables in the sunniest corner of the garden. There was a space in the centre between Michael Selassie and Imogene Carnegie on the far side. Michael took Fiona's hand to help her step over the bench to sit down.

The waiter arrived and handed out menus.

'Is there anything suitable for diabetics?' Estelle

demanded.

'There are two options indicated with an asterisk, madame.'

'Oh yes, I see.'

Once everyone had placed their orders, Fiona turned to Imogene and asked, 'What did you think of Jane's house?'

It was her brother who answered. 'Fascinating place. Did you see those handwritten music books on the piano? Jane wrote those herself, you know.'

'I hadn't realised she actually composed her own music.'

'What came as a surprise to me was that although Jane had written the manuscripts of her first three novels when she lived in the parsonage, it wasn't until she came to Chawton that they were actually published.'

It took some time for the food to arrive and several people decided to take the opportunity to use the facilities.

Estelle was the last to return to the table wearing a particularly grim expression.

'Is anything wrong?' Fiona asked.

'I couldn't find the light switch for that outside toilet and it's pitch black when you close the door. There was no way I could check my blood sugar levels or see to measure my insulin dose. I had to go inside, even then there was a queue. I was forced to have to inject myself by the sinks in case my meal was getting cold. They really should have more cubicles.'

'Oh dear,' Fiona did her best to sound sympathetic. 'Never mind. As you can see, we're all still waiting, so no problem.'

'I must admit, I'm getting quite peckish,' said Franklin.

'You're in luck. I think those two are heading in our direction.'

'Sea bass?' asked the waiter.

'One here,' said Franklin.

'And the other's mine.'

Fiona claimed her duck and Michael the venison from the other waiter.

'Do start. Don't wait for ours to arrive,' insisted Piers.

'I was a bit concerned the vegetarians wouldn't find anything on the menu, but you two have both managed to choose something different.'

'It used to be a problem, although most places would always rustle up an omelette. Nowadays eateries are more used to providing vegetarian options.' Piers' smile made up for Imogene's tight-lipped expression.

As the meal progressed, Fiona realised that she was sitting between the only two people at the table who weren't contributing to the general conversation. Whenever she tried to speak to Imogene, all she received was a curt one-word answer. The woman had chattered away freely the previous evening and she'd seemed perfectly friendly with the others all morning. Quite what Fiona had done to receive such cold shoulder treatment, she had no idea.

On her left, the solemn faced Michael appeared equally distant, totally engaged in his own thoughts, but then he was never one who socialised with anyone. As far as Fiona was aware, he'd shown little interest in the morning's visit. Anyone less like someone on holiday it would be hard to find. He may not have paid much attention to the items on display, but whenever she'd spotted him, his eyes had been constantly on the move taking in every detail of what was happening. Estelle had introduced him as her secretary, but in Fiona's estimation, he appeared to be her bodyguard; ever on the *qui vive* for danger. Now she was being fanciful. What possible danger could there be to threaten Estelle?

At the end of the meal as they were drinking their coffee, Estelle took the opportunity to use the toilet.

'Selassie. Isn't that an Ethiopian name?'

At first, Michael made no response to Renée's question.

'I beg your pardon. I did not appreciate that you were talking to me.'

Renée repeated her question.

'It is, but I am from an ex-French colony.'

'Not the same country as where the president was assassinated last month, I hope? That was a bad business.' Franklin shook his head.

'Indeed.'

'The rioting and unrest are still going on last time I heard.'

The conversation was brought to a sudden halt by a noisy disturbance over by the toilet. Everyone turned to look.

Though the women were too far away for their conversation to be heard, Erma Mahoney was shaking her fist in Estelle's face. As Erma's tirade went on, Estelle stared back at the excited woman, a faint smile on her lips.

A moment later, Erma turned on her heel and marched back inside.

'I wonder what that was all about?' said Piers.

'Probably best not to ask,' Fiona replied.

The coach turned off the road and as they drove up the long gravel drive, the full splendour of the magnificent Elizabethan manor house came into view.

'Wow. I thought we were supposed to be visiting a library not a grand manor house,' said Kathleen.

'It is rather impressive, isn't it? Chawton House was the home of Jane's brother Edward who as you now know was adopted by Thomas and Jane Knight. This house has belonged to the Knight family since the 1500s,' Fiona explained. 'As the guide told us this morning, the cottage he gave to his mother and sister was part of the estate.'

'Richard Knight still lives here though the house is now owned by a foundation and run as a trust,' added Madison.

The coach slowed to a stop halfway down in front of a set of iron work gates. To their right was a short narrow path to the parish church and on their left was a wide gravel road towards what looked as though they might be farm buildings.

'As I mentioned earlier, we are going to begin with a garden tour and our guide has suggested that we meet at this spot. If you'd all like to make your way off the coach, I expect he will be here soon.'

He arrived as Winston executed a perfect three-point turn ready to drive back to the car park in the village.

'Alan Wilson. Pleased to meet you.'

They shook hands.

'I'm Fiona Mason with the Super Sun party.'

'If you'd all like to gather round. Good afternoon and welcome to Chawton House. I'm Alan and I'm one of the garden guides here at Chawton and before you go into the house, I'm going to take you to see one of our garden trails. Now I understand that you are all Jane Austen fans so today we are going to follow the Jane Austen Garden Trail. I suggested we meet here, and not up at the house because our first marker is just over here in front of the hedge.'

Already Franklin had wandered off to the lychgate at the entrance to the church yard. Fiona went after him.

'Don't worry. You will have plenty of time to look round the church later. If you don't come now you are going to get left behind. The rest of the group are already making their way up the drive towards the house.'

Each of the trail markers was marked with a tree stump holding a plaque with an appropriate quotation from one of Jane's novels. The trail led around the side of the house and up onto the attractive library terrace. The group spent a few minutes on the terrace and the cameras clicked away.

'Time to move on everyone,' Alan called out. 'We're going up here and onto the Serpentine Walk where you'll be able to get some great photos of both the house and St Nicholas Church from the Upper Terrace.'

After the first few markers, the group began to spread out a little as one or two people went to examine flowers and others lingered, no longer bothering to listen to the guide's occasional comments.

Fiona stood waiting for Piers and Imogene who were engrossed in their analysis of one of the quotations. Imogene was quite insistent that Piers should take photos of all the quotes printed on the many ceramic oval plaques.

'I don't like to hurry you two, but everyone else has gone into the walled garden. I think we need to catch them up.'

'Oops. Sorry Miss.' Piers gave her a cheeky grin.

As the three of them approached the tall iron gateway, Fiona could hear strident voices on the far side of the wall. Estelle and Michael, standing to the left of the gate, glared at the three latecomers. After a brief pause, Piers and Imogene hurried on to catch up with the rest of the party.

Fiona turned to the African couple with a smile, 'Everything okay?'

'Perfectly fine, thank you, Fiona,' Estelle said crisply.

Resisting the impulse to ask them to join the rest of the group, Fiona moved on. As long as they didn't upset anyone else, the pair could stay there.

There was still thirty-five minutes left at the end of their garden tour before they were due to gather at the entrance to meet the house guide.

'By all means, enjoy the gardens at your leisure in the meantime, but if you decide to go for a quick cup of tea in the café, please do keep an eye on the time. With luck, because it is low season, the queue shouldn't be too long, but you cannot afford to be late. The tour will begin promptly at three o'clock and our guide won't wait and you'll miss the chance to see round the house.'

As her passengers began to drift away, Fiona turned to Madison. 'Have you decided what you would like to do?'

'If it's alright with you, I'd like to go back to the terrace garden and take a few more photos.'

'No problem. I'll see you at the meeting point.'

Fiona breathed a sigh of relief. Even though Madison was working hard not to put a foot wrong today, the last thing Fiona wanted was having to try and make polite conversation with the girl.

Chapter 7

Fiona checked her watch. Two minutes to go. Their guide was already waiting and though Michael was standing at the back of one of the small clusters of people waiting by the entrance, there was still no sign of Estelle.

A distant clock struck the hour. A full minute later Estelle appeared from round a corner strolling nonchalantly towards them. Fiona noticed she kept rubbing the back of her right shoulder, a pained expression on her face.

Their guide led them through the entrance lobby and into the grand hall. Coming in from the bright sunlight outside, it took a moment for Fiona's eyes to adjust before she could appreciate the rich dark wood panelling and the deep ruby red curtains and furnishings. She listened with only half an ear to the guide's history of the house, much of which their garden guide had already told them.

She moved to the display stand detailing the owners of the house from 1580, when it was first built by John Knight, up to the time when Jane's brother Edward inherited the house in 1794. She was so engrossed reading the details that it was several minutes before she realised everyone had moved over to the stone fireplace to examine the line of small wooden shields which according to the guide, were family crests.

Fiona wasn't the only one who had not gravitated to the far side of the room to listen to the guide's explanation. Estelle was leaning on the octagonal table in the window bay a few feet away still rubbing her shoulder.

'Is everything all right?'

Estelle blinked rapidly. 'I think I've been stung by a wasp or something. It's made me a trifle dizzy.'

'Would you like to go back and sit in the coach? I can

easily ring Winston to come and fetch you.'

Estelle jerked herself upright and said sharply, 'Oh no. I shall be fine. Please do not fuss.'

Fiona swallowed the comment she was about to make, deciding it was probably best to simply smile and leave the woman to join the others when she felt ready.

Though nothing more had been said about their altercation, Erma appeared to be keeping her distance from Estelle. She'd worn a tight-lipped expression ever since, although Estelle appeared to have forgotten all about it.

Some five minutes later, the group was ready to move on.

'If there are no more questions, follow me and we'll go up to the dining room.'

Fiona glanced round to check on Estelle who was still standing by the table, one hand resting on the back of a chair. Their eyes met. Estelle immediately drew herself up to her full height and taking slow but determined steps, crossed to the short flight of stairs. Swathed in her long African robes and turban, the statuesque woman cut a commanding figure. It was as though she was putting on an act for Fiona's benefit. The words of an old Joyce Grenfell song came into her mind; "Stately as a galleon, she sailed across the floor". Fiona felt uneasy but she wasn't sure why.

Michael was also watching Estelle's progress. He had hung back and apart from Fiona; Michael was the last to leave the room. Perhaps the performance had been intended to impress him and not her. It was probably no more than Estelle's attempt to distance herself from Michael who had been so assiduous in following in her footsteps like some kind of guard dog all morning.

Fiona lost sight of Estelle as everyone trooped up the half dozen steps and along the panelled corridor to the next room.

Like the Great Hall, the dining room featured dark wood panels and ruby red curtains. In the centre was a long wooden table.

'This large table is the very one where Jane Austen would have sat when she came to dine. Jane wrote about the many wonderful evenings she spent at Chawton House having dinner with her brother and his family in several of her letters,' said their guide as she lovingly stroked the dark wood. 'If you are a Jane Austen fan as I am, then this room with all its memories has a special atmosphere.'

Each of the dozen place settings at the table had a small name card. At the head of the table sat Edward Austen Knight, with their mother at the far end. Jane's place was in the centre on one side with her back to the window. To her right was her favourite niece and great friend and confidante, Fanny Knight. Jane's sister Cassandra sat next but one on her left adjacent to her brother Edward.

It was inevitable that all the women in the party wanted to be photographed sitting in Jane's chair even though the guide pointed out that the allocated place settings followed the typical arrangements of that period and were not based on any documented evidence. Imogene caused a few smiles when she insisted on sitting on every chair at the table to ensure she sat in the exact same chair that Jane had once used.

Eventually their guide was able to lead them over to a corner display case at the far end of the room. 'The suit of clothes on this model belonged to Edward. As you can see, it's a very similar design to the one you see him wearing in the large portrait alongside with the same yellow breeches. Many of the young men of the time had such portraits painted to celebrate them making the Grand Tour of Europe. That's why he's looking so regal, casually leaning on his walking cane. He wrote a diary of his journey and you can see it in the display here below.'

It was quite cramped in the corner and impossible for everyone to see at once so Fiona hung back and went to look at the other portraits hung around the room. She was leaning over the piano to read the inscription below the painting of Edward's wife and children when a sudden cry made everyone turn to see what was going on.

'There's no need to push me out of the way.'

Imogene was glaring at Estelle.

'Then you shouldn't hog the view.'

Imogene was perhaps the most ardent Austen fan in the group, but she did have a tendency to lean over the smaller exhibits and read every detail which made it difficult for the others. Fiona had noticed it earlier when they had been at the small museum before lunch.

'I was trying to read the diary,' Imogene protested.

It wasn't Fiona but their guide who was the first to step in to avert an unpleasant scene. 'Ladies and gentlemen, there is still much to see, let's move on. We are going up to the Oak Room on the first floor.'

As everyone began to file out, Michael marched over to Estelle who pulled away as he tried to take her arm. She took a few unsteady steps towards the door.

'That woman's been drinking again,' someone muttered behind Fiona. 'You can bet it was vodka not water in that bottle she was drinking from earlier.'

Imogene was still complaining about the incident to her brother by the time they reached the Oak Room. She was soon distracted when the guide pointed out a deep alcove in a window bay looking out over the long drive up to the house.

'This is where Jane loved to sit either reading or sewing on her many visits here.'

It was no surprise when Imogene insisted Piers took her photo seated in the easy chair even though there was no evidence that it was the same chair that Jane had used. It was then Piers' turn. Several of the book club members decided that they too would have their pictures taken.

Inevitably the process took some time, but another of the room's attractions was a collection of period dresses much to the delight of the ladies in the group.

In the end, the guide had to clap her hands to get everyone's attention. 'Before we move on, I'd like to point out some of the paintings in here.'

'They're all women,' said Renée.

'Exactly,' the guide continued. 'Remember I said before, this building was bought with the intention of making it the Centre of Early Women's Writing. Both in here and particularly in the Long Gallery where we're going next, the portraits are of 18th century women writers such as Mary Knowles, Amelia Opie and Marie Robinson who were well known in their day. Jane Austen would have been familiar with their work and they would have influenced her own writing. The aim of this centre is to help rediscover these lost women writers so that they can be appreciated today. However, before we leave this room, there is one name you probably will recognise though not for her writing.'

She led the way over to the picture that Fiona had been looking at previously, the one that had seemed familiar.

'This is Georgiana Cavendish, Duchess of Devonshire.'

'Wasn't there a film about her recently?' asked Kathleen.

'I believe so. The Duchess was of course famous as a great socialite, a style icon and political activist, but what is perhaps not so well known is that in her day, she was also a much-read novelist and a poet.'

The group formed a crocodile along the gallery towards the so-called Tapestry Room.

'Sadly, when the family fell on hard times at the beginning of the last century, along with so many of the precious objects in the house, all the tapestries had to be sold off, but we still have this magnificent painting of the house as it was in 1740. Instead of the exposed red brickwork we see on the outside of the house today, back then, as the painting shows, it was covered with a whitewashed render. Other than that, the house appears much the same as it does today.'

'Wasn't there a smaller version of that painting in the Jane Austen House?' asked Ruth Lloyd. 'If not a copy then one very similar.'

'You're right,' agreed June Summerhayes. 'It was in the

vestibule.'

Apart from the painting, there was much to look at. Two painting easels held large, illustrated display boards, one headed "The Chawton landscape", describing the picture and the changes made by Edward and his predecessor. Both men favoured the more natural landscape fashionable at the time. The other board held a fascinating account of Jane Austen's England.

More so than the passengers on her usual tour groups, it was clear that members of Super Sun's Footsteps Tours were keen to read almost all of the plentiful written information to learn as much as possible about one of their well-loved authors. Even Franklin and Renée appeared engrossed on the panel on Jane Austen and her times.

On the other side of the room, separated by a central staircase coming up from the floor below, was a narrow, raised platform. Along its backwall was an enormous folding screen. It was a good three metres tall and seven metres long. Fiona was not the only one to be fascinated by the map of 18th century Georgian London portrayed on it. She was so engrossed examining the tiny ships drawn in the wide serpent-like shape of the River Thames that it was only when she heard laughter coming from the next room, she realised the guide had moved on. Fiona was by no means the only one left behind, but it appeared their guide was no longer bothering to wait before beginning her spiel. Perhaps the woman wasn't used to groups who wanted to pore over every exhibit.

Fiona took a quick look round and decided that if the guide wasn't bothering to usher on the stragglers, neither would she. If they no longer wished to listen, it was their choice.

'My poor brain is beginning to suffer from information overload,' Kathleen confided as Fiona caught up with her at one of the long tables with a display of open books.

Fiona chuckled. 'I know the feeling. There is so much to take in, isn't there? But I think we're nearly at the end now.'

'When the guide said that the theme of this year's exhibition was 'Man up!' I can't say I was much interested, but in fact it's all quite fascinating isn't it. I had no idea so many women decided to dress as men and went into the military or became pirates. I heard the guide say that the next room is all about writers, but I think I'm just going to take photos of all the information panels and read them later.'

The Grand Staircase led down to the tiny gift shop.

'Ladies and gentlemen, this is where I leave you, but before you go, there is one more room to see.'

The guide knocked on a large wooden door. There was the sound of a key being turned and they were invited in by a grey-haired, bespectacled man.

Once they were all inside, he closed the door and turned to face them.

'Good afternoon Everyone and welcome to Chawton House Library. Back in Jane Austen's day, this would have been the parlour, but it was converted into a library in the 1870s. Today the library has a collection of over nine thousand books plus related original manuscripts which, as you are by now well aware, focus on women's writing from 1600 to 1830. The library's main aim is to promote and facilitate study in this field and it works in partnership with the University of Southampton. The collection includes over five thousand books that came from the Knight Family held originally in the library at Godmersham Park, Edward Knight's main residence near Canterbury.'

The room was lined with bookshelves from floor to ceiling, but even so it was evident that the room was far too small to hold so many books.

'But...'

Before Franklin could state the obvious, the man continued, 'Here in this room, we have roughly only two thousand books on the shelves and the rest, including the earliest and most valuable books, are kept in the underground archives. Now before you look around, let me show you this.'

He moved over to one of the bookshelves and everyone dutifully shifted in the crowded space to be able to see.

'At first glance, this may look like an ordinary set of books but…' he paused for effect. 'If I press here, you'll see it opens to reveal a small secret hidey hole. It was added in the 20th century by the last member of the Knight family to own the house. It seems Richard may have been a bit of a tippler, and this is where he hid a bottle of his favourite whisky and a glass.'

There was a gentle titter before everyone began examining the shelves for themselves.

Their tour now at an end, everyone was free to go their separate ways for the next hour or so to look around the shop, take tea in what had been the old kitchen or explore more of the gardens or visit the church halfway down the drive.

Fiona waited a few moments in case anyone had any questions and Madison dutifully came over to join her.

'That went well, I think. Everyone seemed to enjoy themselves.'

Fiona smiled. 'I certainly hope so. Have you decided what you would like to do now?'

'If it's alright with you, I promised I'd take Piers and Imogene to see where Jane's mother and sister Cassandra are buried in the church yard.'

'Of course, it is.'

Fiona was busy chatting with Anthony and Kathleen Trueman as they waited for the coach, when she noticed a worried-looking Michael hovering a few feet away, obviously anxious to speak to her.

'Is something wrong?'

'It's Madame du Plessis. She appears to be missing.'

'There's still a few minutes. The coach isn't here yet. Let's face it Estelle is not the best time-keeper in the group.'

He shook his head. 'But she's been missing for the last couple of hours. She didn't come into the library. When we all went in and the door was closed, I looked around and realised she was missing. I assumed that she had lagged behind somewhere.'

'Are you sure? It was very crowded in that small room. It was difficult, but I thought I'd counted everyone in. I was the last and I didn't notice anyone lingering in the shop.'

'She definitely was not there. I have been searching everywhere, the house and the garden. I went right down to the wilderness, but she is nowhere to be seen.'

'I've just come from the church and she wasn't in there. Let's ask the others if they've seen her.' Fiona clapped her hands for attention.

Twenty minutes after the coach was due to depart, there was still no sign of Estelle.

Chapter 8

'You do not understand. I cannot leave without her.'

'Mr Selassie!' Fiona took a deep breath and slowly counted to ten. 'Michael, there is absolutely nothing to be gained by you remaining here. The whole place has been searched. Estelle du Plessis is not here. What possible good can it do for you to remain? You have no transport. Come back with us now on the coach and we will report her disappearance to the police.'

'No.' His eyes widened in alarm.

'Get on the coach before I…'

'I meant no police.'

Michael hesitated a moment, then turned and mounted the steps onto the coach.

By the time the coach pulled up outside their hotel, Fiona had regained her composure, but she remained in her seat as the passengers silently filed past her. It was only then she realised that the coach had been eerily quiet for the whole twenty-five-minute drive back without the usual hum of excited chatter. There was a decided tension in the air.

She watched Winston help the elderly Anthony Trueman down the steps and turned her head to look for Michael. He was still sitting on the back seat, arms folded, his eyes hooded but otherwise his face expressionless.

'Winston needs to take the coach to the car park.'

He glared at her, got to his feet and stomped down the aisle and followed her off the coach.

'Why don't you want the police informed?'

'You do not understand.'

'Then explain it to me.'

He stood his ground, but when he realised that she would

not give way, he relented with a long sigh.

'Not out here. Let's go inside and find somewhere quiet.'

Once they were ensconced in two large bucket seats in a quiet corner of the deserted lounge, she waited for him to begin.

'It is complicated.'

'I'm listening, Michael.'

He gave a deep sigh. 'My name is not Michael Selassie and I am not a tourist.'

'That comes as no surprise. Neither are you Estelle's secretary.'

'No.'

'Are you worried that she has been abducted?'

He looked surprised. 'Why would anyone do that?'

'Then if you are not her bodyguard, why are you here?'

He shook his head.

'I presume Estelle is also travelling under a false name.'

He nodded. 'Is that why you do not wish to report her disappearance to the police?'

When it looked like he would say no more, she asked, 'Is her disappearance anything to do with the argument you were having in the grounds earlier.'

His jaw tightened.

She sat back, folded her arms and waited. The minutes ticked by.

'Hah!' he snorted. 'You are a formidable lady.'

'You'd better believe it. And this is going to be a long night as I do not intend to leave this room until I have an explanation.'

He gave a half smile and shook his head.

'I came to England in an attempt to persuade her to return home. When I discovered she'd arranged this holiday, I booked a place also.'

There was a long pause.

'And?'

'That is all I can tell you for the time being. But I can assure you that neither she nor I have done anything illegal.

Neither of us are wanted by the authorities of any nation.'

It was obvious that she would get nothing more out of the man posing as Michael.

'In that case, we will leave it for now. It is possible that she will return of her own accord this evening. After all, I'm assuming her things are still in her room. However, if she has not returned by the end of dinner, as tour manager, I will have no choice but to report her missing.'

He nodded.

~

It was already getting dark in London by the time James Fitzwilliam entered the inner office. It looked like being another late night for both him and the chief.

'You wanted me, sir.'

'Have you seen this latest podcast by the Kinyande Peoples Party?' Montgomery-Jones pushed back the monitor so both men could watch.

'Is that Jakande? I thought the KPP leader was under house arrest.'

'But clearly not silenced. He starts off denouncing the ruling One Nation Party for granting concessions to European and American mining corporations, then there is this.'

He turned up the sound and a deep rich baritone filled the room. The language was French, but the call to action was clear. 'For too long, our government has allowed these faceless foreign capitalists to exploit our precious mineral resources. How much longer will our people continue to work long hours deep in the mineral mines in unhealthy, often dangerous conditions? I ask you, my brothers, who benefits from their toil? Is it the workers?' Jakande shook his head. 'No, my loyal people, *our* Kinyande metals are being taken abroad and all the profits end up in the pockets of these foreigners and their shareholders whilst our noble hardworking men receive a pittance. I ask you, good people of Kinyande, is that just?'

Jakande may have been filmed from a room in his own house but he clearly had a supportive audience who cheered him on. What they lacked in numbers, they made up for in volume.

'The time has come! We must take action and demand this government evict these foreign plunderers or step aside for those who will. People of Kinyande stand behind us and let the whole world know, we will no longer be ground under the heel of an uncaring government for the benefit of faceless capitalists.'

He punched a fist in the air as the cheers rose to a crescendo.

Montgomery-Jones muted the volume.

'Fighting talk,' commented James. 'So much for the proposed British trade deal.'

'Exactly. The government contract was negotiated with Antoine Barbier himself. If his One Nation Party is toppled from power, everything that the Trade Department has achieved in the last six months could be rendered null and void.' Montgomery-Jones shook his head.

'What are the chances of that contract being honoured?'

'At this stage, your guess is as good as mine. Barbier was something of a dictator for all that the country is supposed to be a democratic republic. Apart from his wife, most of his ministers were simply yes men who followed Barbier's bidding. Even if the party remains in power, there are no guarantees his successor will abide by it.'

Montgomery-Jones pushed forward the papers in front of him, put his elbows on his desk, steepling his fingers. A habit James knew well, and which indicated his MI6 chief was worried.

'Surely, even if Jakande's party gains the support of the masses they don't have the military firepower to challenge the government without backing from the neighbouring countries that oppose the ONP's particular brand of Fascism?'

Montgomery-Jones nodded. 'With that I would concur.'

'Not having embassy status in the country makes it doubly difficult to keep track of exactly what is going on.'

'Not to mention discovering the whereabouts of our missing trade delegate. I think it is time you make contact with our stations in the neighbouring countries to see if they can help clarify the picture while I speak again to Jean-Claude in the French Embassy and see what his man in Kinyande can tell us.'

'I'll get onto it straight away, sir.'

'Good man.'

~

The receptionist had promised to ring Fiona if Estelle returned to the hotel under her own steam. Fiona glanced at her watch. She felt more annoyed than worried. From what little she knew of the woman; it was just like her to take herself off without telling anyone. She'd probably got bored with the tour and slipped out into the garden and forgotten the time. Any minute now, Estelle du Plessis would waltz back in completely unapologetic.

Rather than sitting about up in her room, Fiona made her way down to the ground floor. She noticed Kathleen at the front desk talking earnestly to the receptionist.

'Thank you so much. They will appreciate it.' Kathleen turned quickly almost bumping into Fiona coming up behind her.

'I'm so sorry, Fiona'

'My fault entirely. I shouldn't have crept up on you. Is everything okay?'

'Perfectly thank you, dear. I've just been asking the young lady to book an early morning call for Ruth and Erma. They both overslept this morning. I had to give them a ring when they didn't turn up for breakfast. Erma tried to set the alarm on her mobile phone, but it didn't work. I like to keep an eye on the pair of them. Ruth is a little shy, needs taking out of

66

herself. That's why I persuaded her to join the book club. Erma has been a member of our group since it started but her husband died last year, and she's turned into a bit of a recluse. She can be a bit fierce, but she's good hearted really. That's why I'm so pleased they came on this trip. It will be so good for both of them to get away on a little holiday.'

Fiona had to smile. 'It's good of you to look after them.'

'Is there any sign of our missing lady?'

'Not yet.'

'It's obvious poor Michael is really worried. I expect she'll be here soon.'

'I'm sure you're right.'

Back in her room, Fiona kicked off her shoes and sank down on to the bed. Estelle's disappearance was certainly a mystery. Where could the woman possibly have got to? Before they had left Chawton House, the staff had helped check all the buildings and gardens in case she had collapsed somewhere but there had been no sign of the missing woman. As her things were still in her room, there was no indication she had planned to leave the tour. Most puzzling of all, why hadn't Michael wanted her disappearance reported to the police?

Still, there was no point sitting here in useless speculation, she might as well get showered and changed ready for dinner. It was only as she picked up her tote bag from the end of the bed where she'd tossed it earlier that she remembered the letter she'd been given that morning. She retrieved the now crumpled envelope from the bottom of her bag and pulled out a sheet of lined paper torn from a spiral notepad.

In shaky childish capitals it read, YOU ARE A MEAN VINDICTIVE BITCH.

She scrunched it into a ball and aimed it at the waste bin. It hit the side and bounced out again onto the floor.

'Damn.'

Chapter 9

Dinner came and went. Still no Estelle.

'I wonder where she could have got to,' remarked Kathleen.

'Heaven knows, but I have to say it's good to be able to sit and enjoy a meal without having to watch every word you say in case she made some disparaging remark.'

From the sheepish grins from several others at the table, June Summerhayes' acerbic comment met with a great deal of sympathy.

'When Estelle wasn't putting people down, she was lording it over everyone trying to make out she was so much better than the rest of us,' agreed Ruth Lloyd.

'And how!' Fiona tried to give Madison a warning glare, but the girl continued, 'Always banging on about her privileged background. I ask you, who has a governess these days?'

'My sister was a governess,' said Erma sharply. 'Highly trained and much sought after I might add.'

'I'm sure, I didn't mean…' Madison's voice petered out.

Time to intervene. 'This chocolate mousse is excellent, how's your apple and blackberry crumble, Anthony?'

He looked up startled, then smiled at Fiona. 'Not as good as my dear wife makes but most agreeable.'

'Flatterer.' Kathleen gave him an indulgent smile. 'But it is his favourite.'

As the general conversation continued on less contentious grounds, Fiona was able to sit back and relax a little.

As everyone began to move out of the restaurant, Fiona made her way over to the table where Michael was sitting and took the empty seat next to him. Piers and Imogene, the only two others still at the table made a quick, diplomatic exit.

'I have asked reception to ensure that Estelle hasn't left any messages and also to check her room. Her belongings are still there. Before I inform the authorities, are you certain there is nothing more you can tell me?'

He shook his head.

A quarter of an hour later, after the helpful young man behind the reception desk had rung round all the local hospitals to ensure that no one answering Estelle's description had been brought into accident and emergency in the last few hours, Fiona informed Super Sun Head Office.

She was still hesitant about ringing the police. Estelle was a responsible adult, and in all likelihood, they would not respond until she had been missing for at least twenty-four hours. Perhaps she should ask the young man at the desk to try the local taxi firms to see if anyone had tried to book a taxi from the Chawton area this afternoon.

The police arrived shortly before ten o'clock. Fiona was summoned to the front desk. The man in charge introduced himself as Detective Sergeant Sanders.

'A body has been found at Chawton House. There will need to be a formal identification, but we believe it to be that of a member of your party. A Mrs Estelle du Plessis. I understand that you reported her missing.'

Fiona felt a hollow in the pit of her stomach. All the way down in the lift after she'd received the call, she had been steeling herself in anticipation.

'Was it a heart attack?' She knew it was a stupid question. If Estelle had died of natural causes, the police would not have sent a plain clothes officer.

'We will not know the exact cause of death until after the post-mortem. In the meantime, we would like to speak to all of the group who accompanied Mrs du Plessis this afternoon.' The man was giving nothing away.

'But several of them may well have gone to bed.'

'I do appreciate that, Mrs Mason. Interviews will be held first thing tomorrow morning. But I do need to speak to you now and if Mrs du Plessis was travelling with anyone else, I will need to speak to them this evening. To your knowledge, was the lady acquainted with any members of the party prior to the start of the holiday?'

'As far as I know, only Michael Selassie.'

If all the interviews were as combative as hers had been, then she would have a very indignant group of passengers to deal with tomorrow morning. At least they would not be made to feel as guilty and inadequate as Detective Sergeant Sanders had succeeded in doing to her.

Fiona closed her bedroom door with a bang and flung her shoulder bag onto the bed.

'Objectionable little man. Odious, officious, self-important upstart.'

How dare he imply that she had been remiss for losing someone supposedly in her care. It was hardly her fault. She couldn't be expected to keep an eye on every passenger during their free time! And as for failing to report her charge's absence earlier, she could just imagine the response she would have received if she'd phoned the police immediately. It had been hard enough not to get fobbed off by the duty officer when she had phoned at eight-thirty.

She was still seething by the time she'd undressed and was ready for bed.

If she was honest, she was just as angry with herself. He'd had a point when he'd asked why she hadn't noticed that Estelle was no longer in the group by the time they had got to the library. But crammed into that small space and being only five-foot-three with everyone towering above her, there was no way she could count heads.

And why hadn't she kept schtum about the fracas

between Estelle and Madison last evening? She did think twice when he'd asked if there had been any incidents between the missing woman and anyone else in the party. There was little point in hiding the fact that Estelle appeared to delight in upsetting everyone with whom she came in contact. She had mentioned the incident with Madison only because if she hadn't, the policeman would get to hear about it from someone else who might make it sound even worse than it was.

Even that, DS Sanders had implied was due to her failure to keep her assistant under control. Because of his reaction, she decided not to mention the upset with Imogene, the argument Estelle had had with Erma or the raised voices she'd overheard in the garden between her and Michael.

And as for tomorrow! How long would it take to question everyone? What would happen to tomorrow's programme? Perhaps she should at least warn Winston, but was it worth disturbing him at this hour?

'I was wondering if you were going to call this evening.'

'I'm sorry, Peter. I know it's late, but it's been one of those days.'

'I take it you have not been having some kind of late-night party.'

'Anything but! I have just spent the last three-quarters of an hour trying to stop myself from punching a certain DS on the nose.'

There was a long pause at the other end.

'DS as in the initials of one of your passengers or as in police detective?'

'Very much the latter.'

'You are joking, I hope.'

'Sadly not.'

'You had better explain.'

'Remember I told you about the fracas last night? The woman Madison upset, Estelle du Plessis, went missing this afternoon...' It took some time to tell him the full story including the details of her interview.

'But the police are not claiming she was murdered?'

'Not exactly. But why else would they want to know if there had been any problems between her and the rest of the party?'

'I would imagine it was merely standard procedure?'

'But if she just collapsed, why wasn't she found by the people on the next house tour?'

'Obviously, I have no idea, but there must be all sorts of explanations. Perhaps she felt unwell and went back outside for some fresh air and collapsed outside where no one saw her.'

'I will admit it was obvious she wasn't feeling well. At one point I asked her if she wanted to go and find somewhere to sit, but she refused. In any case her body was found in the Tapestry Room by one of the cleaners after all the house tours were finished.'

'Is that what the detective sergeant told you?'

'Not exactly. He asked when I'd seen her last and I said I'd noticed her studying the old map of London. I noticed he raised his eyebrows when I mentioned it was in the tapestry room, so I asked if that was where she'd been found. He didn't deny it.'

'And you put two and two together and made five.'

'Don't be so patronising. I said she must have been hidden otherwise she'd have been found by the next tour. At first, I couldn't think where that might be as there were no large pieces of furniture she could have lain behind, then I remembered there was a second much smaller screen on the landing blocking off a short flight of steps to an office. I remember noticing at the time how it blocked out much of the light from the landing window. When I asked the sergeant if that's where she was found, he ignored me. Nonetheless, he didn't deny it. In fact, his face went bright pink, which confirmed it,' she said indignantly.

'Maybe, but the fact that her body was missed by the visitors who came through after your party does not make it murder.'

'True. But it is suspicious. Why would she have gone behind that screen? The stairs went up to a staff area. There was a big notice at the bottom saying "Chawton House Team Only" to stop visitors.'

'You said the screen was in front of a window, perhaps she wanted to see the view, or more likely if she was feeling unwell, to see if she could open it for some fresh air.'

She gave a derisive snort.

'Fiona,' She could tell by his tone of voice, she was about to get a lecture about leaving well alone and how it was not her place to investigate.

'Anyway,' she interrupted him. 'There's something else rather odd. After Estelle went missing, Michael confessed that neither he nor Estelle are travelling under their real names.'

'Did he explain why?'

'No. I'd already suspected that he wasn't her secretary as Estelle had alleged. I'd assumed from the way he was behaving that he was a bodyguard of some sort. He claimed not. He said he'd come to persuade her to return home.'

'And what do you make of that?'

'At the time, I'd assumed it was because she had run out on her husband and didn't want to be found and Michael had been sent by him to bring her back. But after all that's happened, I'm beginning to wonder if there isn't a great deal more behind it. If that was the situation, why would Michael need to change his name?'

'Please, Fiona. For once, will you leave the investigation to the police? Leave well alone. They will not look kindly on your interference.'

'I am not interfering,' she said indignantly, 'and I don't need a lecture.'

She cut the connection and slammed her mobile down on the bedside table.

Day Three

After the death of Jane's father in 1805, her mother was largely dependent on her sons for her upkeep and that of her two daughters. It was decided that the three of them would spend the summers visiting her sons and return to rented accommodation in Bath during the winter months.

1806 was a particularly unsettled year and after family visits to Steventon, Clifton, Godmersham and Worthing before returning to Bath, Frank Austen offered the women a more permanent solution. Thanks to his promotion in the Navy, Frank was now earning a good salary and suggested that as his new wife would be lonely when he was away at sea, a sensible solution was for his mother and sisters to keep her company in a house he would rent in Southampton near to the naval dockyard at Portsmouth.

Jane found living in a city a challenge after her country childhood. We know that she and her sister Cassandra spent much time out of doors, promenading along the city walls and taking excursions to the River Itchen and the ruins of Netley Abbey.

The following year Frank took the lease of a large house in Castle Square. Jane took great pleasure in helping her mother plan a new layout for the large garden bounded on one side by the city wall. Jane's experience of local life in Southampton inspired the Portsmouth scenes in Mansfield Park.

Sadly, we can no longer see the house because today Castle Square consists of 20th century housing and a public house called the Juniper Berry now stands on the site where Jane lived. However, we will be able to walk Southampton's ancient city walls, said to be a favourite walking spot for Jane, and explore a few local landmarks well known to her. Before leaving Southampton, we will visit the ruins of Netley Abbey, a medieval Cistercian monastery founded in 1239 which inspired Northanger Abbey.

After lunch, we will visit the 18th century Mompesson House which lies in the heart of Salisbury's Cathedral Close. This elegant townhouse was used as the house of Mrs Jennings during the filming of Sense and Sensibility in 1995 which starred Hugh Grant, Kate Winslet, and Emma Thompson. We will also have private behind-the-scenes access to many of the items including costumes and photographs from the film that formed an earlier exhibition.

Super Sun Executive Travel

Chapter 10

The sky was grey and overcast when Fiona opened the curtains the next morning. She peered out at the wet pavements and gave a deep sigh. As if things weren't bad enough without having to do a walking tour in the rain.

She spotted a man hurrying towards the hotel, tugging the hood of his anorak over his head. He had a newspaper tucked under the other arm. At this angle, it was difficult to see his face, but she was reasonably certain it was Lester Summerhayes, one of the book group. She knew he always liked to buy a paper first thing in the morning. She'd heard him ask the receptionist where he could find the nearest newsagent when the coach party from London had first arrived.

Determined to make the best of things, she pulled the notes for the day's itinerary from the stack of files lying on the table, put them in her tote bag and made her way down to breakfast.

Winston looked up as Fiona slid onto the opposite chair.

'Mornin', sweetheart. How's you? Have they found your missing lady yet?'

She quickly brought him up to date.

'I'll have to ring Head Office this morning. Update them on the situation. I suppose I ought to have rung last night but the shock of it all put everything else out of my mind.' She looked at her watch. 'The office won't be open yet. I don't know if I should wait until I've spoken to the police. What do you think?'

'Don't suppose an hour or so is gonna make much difference.'

'I've no idea when the police intend to interview everyone. The detective sergeant said it would be first thing this morning, but he didn't say what time. Heaven knows when we will be able to leave for Southampton. We may have to cancel the visit altogether – at least for this morning.'

'Let's wait and see. No point getting in a tizzy about it now.' Winston patted her hand.

'True. At least there's no booked guide for the morning. Just a drive round the city, and the walls they can walk on their own, assuming it's not teeming down with rain by then.'

'It'll be fine, sweetheart. According to the forecast, the drizzle will clear up in an hour or so and by the afternoon, we should even have some sunshine. If we do end up setting off late, we can easily adjust the times.'

'I suppose so. If the worst comes to the worst, we'll just have to cut out Southampton altogether and go straight to Mompesson House. At least then, I won't have to worry about making a commentary as we do a panoramic drive through the city.'

'You'll be fine, sweetheart. You and me's done this sort of thing dozens of times.'

'I know but you've always told me what's coming up and what to look for. I'm not sure I'll even recognise the places I'm meant to be pointing out. How am I supposed to show everyone the house where Jane lived when it's no longer there? It was pulled down years ago, replaced by a pub.'

He gave one of his low rumbling chuckles. 'Don't you worry. Have I ever let you down? Just 'cause I ain't done this tour before don't mean I ain't done my homework. I've spoken to the chap what normally does it and got all the gen.'

He lifted a town plan from the seat of the chair next to him and laid it in front of her. 'I's marked the route in red. We come down Castle Square and pass the *Juniper Berry* on the left on the corner here, where I's put a cross. You can't miss it. It's a mock Tudor place, all wood with white plaster.'

'Thank you, Winston. You're a star.'

It was inevitable that Fiona was bombarded with questions as more of her passengers came in for breakfast. Rather than have to explain over and over again, and with a promise to find out the latest information, Fiona asked all those she saw to come down for a meeting half an hour before they'd been due to leave and to pass the message on to anyone who came in later.

She had just finished cleaning her teeth after breakfast when she received a call to say that DS Sanders was in the hotel.

'He asked if it would be convenient for you to have a word with him now?' asked the diplomatic voice at the reception desk.

Fiona doubted that the policeman's 'request' had been couched in those words.

'Tell him that I'll come down straightaway.'

The policeman actually smiled as Fiona walked towards him and his colleague. She had to admit he appeared a great deal more relaxed than at their previous encounter.

'I have already spoken to Madison Clark this morning. I understand from her that you have planned a visit to Southampton today.'

'That is what is on the itinerary, but I have asked everyone to come for a meeting at nine o'clock, half an hour before we are scheduled to leave, in order to update them on the arrangements.'

'Perfect.' His smile appeared quite genuine. 'In that case, may I come along and have a word with them all?'

'By all means.'

If nothing else, it would save her from having to tell everyone what had happened when she was unsure just how much she should say. He could also field all the inevitable questions.

'Things might change as new information comes to light and we may need to ask further questions, but at this stage all we need to ascertain is when each of her fellow passengers last saw Mrs du Plessis and ask a few general questions. I doubt it will take long. I see no reason why there should be any delay to your departure.'

'That is excellent news. I'll let the coach driver know straight away.' Fiona felt as though a great weight had been lifted from her shoulders. She was tempted to ask if any progress had been made on the case, but best not to push her luck. Perhaps Estelle's death had been natural causes after all, and the police were simply covering all the bases.

There was a definite spring in her step as she hurried up the first flight of stairs back to her room. Perhaps Peter had been right when he'd suggested that Estelle had gone to see if she could open the window for some fresh air and had collapsed. Her elation did not last for long. Though she had no real idea how long it took to conduct a post-mortem it was highly unlikely that the pathologist had had time to determine the cause of death, especially if it involved tests for drugs or poisons.

There was another explanation, but not one Fiona wanted to contemplate. If DS Sanders had spoken to Madison, had the girl confessed? She put a hand on the banister and steadied herself. No. The idea was ridiculous. Madison had reacted badly to Estelle's put down in front of everyone else and she had a temper, but murder!

She was being fanciful. Why did she have to think the worst?

Fiona was on edge as she waited for the group to gather in the lobby. It wasn't until Madison stepped out of the lift with Kathleen and Anthony Trueman that Fiona appreciated that she'd been standing with her hands clenched so tightly that her nails had dug deep into her palms.

One person who was not there was Michael Selassie. Not that she expected to see him. By his own admission, he had only booked on the tour because he was trying to trace Estelle.

'If we're all here, shall we move into the lounge where it

will be a little quieter.'

DS Sanders was already waiting for them.

To give him his due, he handled the situation well.

'Ladies and gentlemen, I am sure you are all anxious to know what has happened to Mrs du Plessis who went missing on your tour yesterday. I am sorry to have to tell you that the lady has died.'

He but up his hands to quieten the outbreak of exclamations of surprise and inevitable questions.

'Was it a heart attack?'

'A stroke?'

'I am sorry I cannot tell you exactly how she died. That is in the hands of the coroner and it will be some time until all the test results are available, and the exact cause of death can be established.'

There was another noisy buzz of chatter which this time he had to quell by clapping his hands.

'In the meantime, ladies and gentlemen, if would help us to tie up a few loose ends if you would all think back to when you all last remember seeing Mrs du Plessis.'

'She was standing next to me when we were all gathered round the table in the dining room,' volunteered Ruth Lloyd.

'And she was rude to Imogene when you were looking at Edward's Grand Tour notebooks in the corner of the room, wasn't she?' Piers turned to his sister who gave him a very un-sisterly glower.

Heads nodded. That scene between the two women had not gone unnoticed.

'Did anyone see her after that?' asked the detective sergeant.

'She asked if I would take her photo in the Oak Room. There's a little alcove where Jane Austen was supposed to have sat reading by the light of a pretty, mullioned window looking down the drive. Most of us took it in turns to sit there and have our pictures taken,' said Franklin Austin.

'Was the Oak Room before or after the one with that great long map in?' asked Anthony Trueman. 'I can't remember, but Estelle was definitely looking at it.'

'The Tapestry Room. And do you remember if you left the room before her or after.'

Anthony shook his head. 'No idea, I'm sorry.'

'Does anyone else remember seeing her in the Tapestry Room?'

Three or four hands went up.

'Did any of you see her leave?'

'I remember seeing her sitting on that big chest. She didn't look at all well,' said June. 'There were still half a dozen people still in there when we left but I can't say if she was one of them.

'Not to worry.' DS Sanders smiled. 'I believe the next rooms on the tour were the two exhibition rooms and the Library downstairs. Did anyone notice her in any of those?'

The only response was glum looks and shakes of the head.

'Not in the shop perhaps at the end of your tour?'

Again, the response was negative.

'In that case, ladies and gentlemen, we will leave it at that. Thank you all for your time and I trust you will enjoy the rest of your itinerary.'

There was still ten minutes before they were due to leave the hotel and almost everyone left the lounge to return to their rooms. A few of the book club people had brought down all they would need for the day as had Madison. As the friends moved chairs to talk to one another, Fiona smiled at Madison and went over to join her.

'How was your interview with DS Sanders?'

'Fine. He asked the same as he asked everyone else just now. When I'd last seen Estelle.'

'Is that all?'

'He did ask what I thought of her. I told him she was a difficult woman. Acted like some sort of royalty the way she tried to lord it over everyone else. I told him what happened on that first evening at the meet-and-greet when she was drunk.'

'Oh?'

'Did you notice, when we went to that pub restaurant at lunch yesterday, she went out to the bar and bought herself a glass of wine?'

'I believe several other of our guests did the same thing. It's not unusual for people to have a glass of wine with their meal. Especially when they are on holiday.'

Madison pursed her lips in disapproval. 'But they know when to stop.'

'Did you see her have more than one glass?'

'No but…'

'Is that all you told the DS?'

'I did explain how I wasn't the only one she upset.'

'Really? Who else was there?'

'The Canadian woman.'

'Renée.'

Madison nodded. 'The pair of them were having a heck of a spat in the garden at the Jane Austen House Museum before lunch.'

'Do you know what it was about?'

'Not a clue. I was too far away. Besides, I made a point of keeping my distance from that obnoxious woman as much as possible all day yesterday.'

Fiona had to admit she had noticed that after her apology, Madison had given Estelle a wide berth.

Chapter 11

Peter Montgomery-Jones looked up as James burst through the door without waiting for a response to his token rap.

'Reports are coming through that the head offices of the United Metals Corporation have been blown up. There are pictures all over social media.'

'So I see.'

James moved round to Montgomery-Jones' side of the desk and both men stared at the pictures on the PC monitor. Each YouTube video appeared more graphic than the last with scenes of fire raging through the collapsing building.

'That had to be the result of a hell of a lot more than a few Molotov cocktails thrown through the windows.'

For once, Montgomery-Jones failed to raise a disapproving eyebrow at his assistant's choice of language.

'I agree. Which poses the question of where a group of so-called rebel workers got hold of the firepower and the expertise to carry out an operation that reduced a substantial ten-storey building almost to rubble.' Montgomery-Jones leant forward elbows on the desk tapping his chin with the tip of a pencil.

'Any ideas, sir?'

Montgomery-Jones sighed. 'Several spring to mind. However, I do not think we should attempt to lay the blame on Xavier Jakande and his Kinyande Peoples Party too soon.'

'You think it could be a rival in the governing ONP. An attempt to make Vannier look ineffective as a leader.'

'That is a definite possibility. It will be interesting to see if by tomorrow morning there are calls for him to resign.'

Montgomery-Jones tapped his keyboard.

'As I thought. It appears that this is not an isolated

incident. It seems there have been attacks, admittedly so far less spectacular, on other foreign head offices, one American and two French. Jubilant mobs are rampaging through the city and the military appear to have lost control.'

'The capital is in chaos.' James' voice was barely above a whisper.

'I see the Foreign Office has responded by recommending that all British nationals working in the country and their families return to Britain while the airports are still working.'

James shook his head. 'Assuming that's even possible. The situation is getting worse by the minute.'

'No more news about our missing member from the trade delegation, I presume?'

'Not yet and this situation isn't going to help matters.'

'Indeed.'

~

Even though the worst of the early morning rush hour traffic was over, the coach made slow progress getting out of the city, but once they reached the motorway there were no holdups and they hit the outskirts of Southampton in just under half an hour.

Madison took the same seat towards the back of the coach that she'd had the day before. Fiona felt a little guilty that she hadn't asked the girl to join her, but she had far too much on her mind to have to make small talk.

The low buzz of excited chatter filled the coach behind her. It didn't take much to guess what they were all speculating about. Every now and then she caught snatches of the exchange between Kathleen and Anthony in the seat behind her.

'…why do you think he was so keen to know …'

Anthony's voice was much softer, and Fiona couldn't hear his reply.

'But the police must know where her body was found.'

It was a question that Fiona had been wondering since she'd lain in bed after her own interview with DS Sanders. She still didn't have an answer. Was he trying to find who had seen her last or did it imply that the police didn't think that Estelle had died where her body had been found? Either way, it was beginning to sound as if the death was suspicious.

But who would want to kill Estelle? What was even more disconcerting was the fact that tours of Chawton House were strictly controlled. No one could look round the house except with a guide. The only logical explanation was that if Estelle was murdered it had to be one of her own party.

For the second time that day, Fiona told herself to stop letting her imagination run away with her. Estelle died of natural causes. Time to think about something else.

She pulled her tour instructions folder from her tote bag and checked the tour manager's duties for the trip. It was only a ten-minute walk from the coach drop-off point to the steps up to the top of the famous walls. There were a couple of features associated with Jane Austen that she needed to point out along the way, but once they reached the entrance, passengers were free to climb to the top or do their own thing for an hour or so.

She'd walked the walls at Southampton several times before. Perhaps instead, she could hit the shops and see if she could see anything suitable to buy the grandchildren for Christmas. If she wanted to save money on postage to Canada by sending them by sea, the last date for posting was now only weeks away.

Winston's predictions about the weather were spot on and the sun was shining in an almost clear sky by the time the coach approached the ancient city of Salisbury, an important centre dating back to pre-Roman times.

The road outside Mompesson House was too narrow to allow the coach to drop them off in the Cathedral Close itself and the party had to walk the last few hundred yards to Choristers Square.

'We are still a little early for our tour but if you would all wait out here a moment, I'll go and see if they are ready for us,' Fiona instructed.

Once they were all inside, they were welcomed by a spritely lady, well into her retirement, with bouncy grey curls and a merry twinkle in her eyes.

'Good afternoon everyone and welcome. I'm Eleanor, one of the volunteer guides here at Mompesson House and I understand that you folk, like me, have something of a passion for Jane Austen. All of our rooms are arranged to look exactly as the house would have been at the turn of the 18th century back in Jane Austen's time.'

'Did Jane ever visit the house?'

Eleanor gave a big grin and gave an exaggerated shrug of her shoulders. 'Well it is possible that Jane visited the Portman sisters who lived here at the time, but there is no record of her ever having done so. Though I love to think that she did, if I'm honest, I think that possibility is pretty remote.'

Eleanor's enthusiasm was infectious as she led them through the house describing the scenes from the famous 1995 film of *Sense and Sensibility* shot in each room.

'I can just imagine Mrs Jennings having tea in here,' said Piers as they surveyed the drawing room.

'Of course, in the novel, Jane locates Mrs Jennings' house in London, but Mompesson is typical of elegant townhouses of that period. And now let me show you some of the costumes and photographs from the film that we still have from our major exhibition displayed not long after the film was released.'

At the end of their tour, they all went into the garden.

'Considering we're right in the centre of a major city, it's surprisingly large isn't it?' remarked Kathleen. 'It even has a lovely little arbour with a café area at the bottom there.'

It wasn't long before the majority of the party drifted down to the cafe.

By the time Fiona joined them, most of them were deep in conversation about the film.

'It was a super movie. It won no end of awards including best picture. It had so many famous actors in it – Emma Thompson, Kate Winslet and Hugh Grant,' enthused Erma, one of the normally quiet book club ladies.

'Didn't Emma Thompson write the screenplay as well?' asked her friend Ruth.

'And Alan Rickman played Colonel Brandon. I loved him. One of my favourite actors,' said Kathleen. 'Did you see the film, Madison?'

'It came out several years before I was born.'

'Of course, silly me. What about when they showed it on television? Surely you saw that?'

Madison shook her head.

'I suppose even that was some time ago now.' Kathleen gave a sigh and took a long sip of her coffee.

Madison must have sensed the woman's regret at the swift passage of time, because she said brightly, 'I do know the film contributed to the resurgence in the popularity of Jane Austen's books. As I said in my talk the other day, Jane may hold the accolade of being the world's favourite woman writer, but it's only in the last thirty to forty years that she has become so well known.'

'Much as I hate to break up the conversation, people,' Fiona interrupted, 'but I think we need to be making tracks soon. Winston will be waiting.'

As they all wound their way along the Cathedral Close and back to the High Street, Fiona fell into step alongside Madison.

'Actually, I managed to get hold of a DVD of the film. I bought it before I was told you were going to be joining us. I was going to show it in place of one of the lectures.'

'Did you bring it with you?'

Fiona nodded.

'Then let's show it tonight. It was obviously such a hit

with them all, I'm sure they'd all love to see it again, especially as so much of it was shot here at Mompesson House. I can always do my lecture another night.' Madison was all smiles.

'Well let's ask everyone when we get back on the coach and see what they would like to do.'

Fiona felt a surge of relief. Although Madison's first talk had gone reasonably well, having seen the girl's notes for her lecture on Feminism and Jane Austen, she'd been wondering just how she could persuade Madison to let her show the film instead of the lecture. Things had gone even better than she'd anticipated.

Fiona dropped her tote bag on the chair and sank down on the bed with a sigh. All in all, it hadn't been such a bad day despite all her misgivings at breakfast. No arguments had broken out and the visit to Mompesson House had been a great success. On the journey back from Salisbury, everyone sounded enthusiastic about what they had seen. The vote to see the film was unanimous. Even the Canadian couple who had admitted earlier that they were not Austen enthusiasts, said how much they had enjoyed seeing all the costumes and were looking forward to seeing the film.

She glanced at her watch. There was still an hour before she needed to change for dinner. This might be a good time to write up the day's report and get it over with. Alternatively, she could put it off till later and go down to the café for a cup of tea.

The buzz of her mobile made the decision for her.

'Peter, how lovely to hear from you. Is there a reason for ringing so early?'

'I am here in the hotel. Are you free to come down and join me in the lounge?'

She could tell by the tone of his voice that this was not a social call.

'I hope you haven't come all this way because you think I can't cope with all the problems by myself.'

'No, not exactly. I am here in an official capacity.'

Her mouth had suddenly gone dry. That sounded ominous. 'I'll be down straight away.'

Chapter 12

Peter Montgomery-Jones was waiting in the lobby when she emerged from the lift. Any lingering thoughts Fiona may have had that he was here to support her were quickly dispersed when she saw him. Not only was he dressed in a grey-striped three-piece suit, the expression on his face, or rather the lack of it, as he walked towards her, told her that their meeting was to be strictly official. No embrace, not even a peck on the cheek, just a quick polite smile.

'Shall we find somewhere to talk.' It wasn't a question.

They walked side by side into the adjacent lounge and he took her to the cluster of armchairs in the far corner half-hidden by one of the many planters of tall leafy indoor plants. Once she was seated, he returned to the small coffee bar near the door and spoke to the young man polishing glasses behind the counter.

'I have ordered a pot of tea for us. I trust that will be satisfactory,' he said on his return.

Such was the authority that the MI6 officer exuded, a tea tray arrived in a couple of minutes despite the fact that there was no waiter service. The man behind the counter had left his post to bring it over.

'I take it you're here because of Estelle du Plessis.'

Although there were a dozen people in the room, most were sitting on the far side alongside the large picture windows, there was little chance of their conversation being overheard.

'I am.'

'Which I assume means she was murdered.'

He raised an eyebrow. 'As for that, I know no more than you. I am not part of that investigation.'

'I don't understand. Then why are you here?'

'As you told me last night, Estelle du Plessis was not the woman's real name. We now know that it was Barbier, Eshe Barbier.'

'You say that as if I should know who that is, but I'm afraid I don't.'

'She was the widow of Antoine Barbier, the President of Kinyande, a small country in Central Africa. He was assassinated at the beginning of the month.'

Fiona felt her eyebrows shoot up towards her hairline. 'I remember reading about it in the paper, but I'd forgotten the name. But what on earth was she doing in Britain?'

'That is something my department would very much like to know.'

'I don't suppose the government establishment are too happy with the death of such a high profile figure on British soil, especially if she was murdered. It won't exactly help diplomatic relations. I assume that's why you're here.'

He didn't answer, simply giving one of his enigmatic smiles.

'What about Michael. Can't he shed any light on what she was doing over here?'

'It appears the man has disappeared.'

'He left the tour after Madame Bardier's death, which is understandable for all sorts of reasons, but I assumed that he'd stayed in Winchester to see to the arrangements for returning her body back home for burial.'

'Indeed.' Peter's expression darkened. 'However, according to the hotel staff, Michael Selassie checked out first thing this morning.'

'Assuming she was murdered, I suppose Michael's disappearance makes him the prime suspect.'

'As to that, as I said, I am not part of the investigation and cannot comment.'

'Michael was using a false name too. I don't think she was that pleased to see him when he turned up on the tour. The last time I spoke to him he claimed he'd followed her to

England to persuade her to return home.'

Fiona's head was spinning. There were so many questions she wanted to ask but even if he knew the answers, as she knew from old, there was no way he would tell her. It had caused such friction between them in the past, but she was determined to try not to let that come between them again. Not now.

'I still don't understand, if you are not taking over the case, what do you hope to find out by coming here? Especially if Michael has disappeared.'

'My intention was to speak to Mr Selassie. However, my visit has allowed me to discuss the situation with the local constabulary and establish the facts.'

Fiona sipped her tea, deep in thought.

'Estelle… or Eshe as I suppose I now have to call her, may not have been too pleased to have Michael dogging her every footstep, but she never gave any impression of being afraid of him. And if his intention had been to kill her, why would he wait twenty-four hours? It doesn't make sense.'

'Are you positive that when Michael spoke to you last evening, he said nothing more than you have told me already? Something that may not have seemed relevant at the time.'

She thought for a moment or two, then shook her head. 'I'm sorry, Peter. I can't think of anything.'

'You mentioned that he too was travelling under a false name.'

She nodded. 'That was why he was so reticent to speak to the police when she first went missing.'

'But he never mentioned his real name or gave you any indication of who he might be?'

'I'm afraid not. All he said was that he'd come to persuade her to return home. I know they had at least one heated discussion an hour or so before she died, but I didn't get the impression that he was threatening her at all. After that they kept their distance even on the tour of the house.'

'Might he have spoken to any of the other passengers

about himself or Eshe Barbier?'

'I very much doubt it. Michael kept himself very much to himself. Do you want me to ask around?'

'No,' he said sharply. 'Please do not involve yourself any further.'

She took a deep breath. 'In which case, I suggest you ask them yourself. But it will have to be tomorrow morning as there will be no time this evening. Right now, everyone will be dressing for dinner and straight after we have eaten, we will be watching a film.'

They stared at each other across the table.

Eventually he said. 'As you wish. First thing tomorrow morning.'

Whatever Peter said, she had no intention of sitting idly by. And what he didn't know, he couldn't complain about.

After the meal was over, everyone moved into the private conference room set aside for their use for the evening talks. One of the hotel staff loaded the DVD into the digital projector system and explained the controls to Madison. Fiona was happy to pass over the responsibility as the girl's technical abilities far exceeded her own. It also left her free to chat with the others as they helped themselves to coffee from the table at the back of the room.

The person who had done the most to get to know her fellow passengers was probably Kathleen. Though her husband was nominally the president of their book group, Fiona had little doubt that it was his motherly wife who made it her mission to make all the members feel welcome and part of the group and that instinct extended to those with whom she was sharing this holiday.

'Milk?' Fiona asked Kathleen, holding up the jug.

'Yes please.' Kathleen proffered her cup. 'Wasn't this afternoon wonderful? Our guide was a real character, wasn't she? She certainly knew her stuff.'

'I think everyone enjoyed it.'

'Oh yes. Including Franklin and Renée who don't know

93

much about Jane Austen at all. They even downloaded a copy of *Sense and Sensibility* onto their Kindle when we got back to the hotel. Can't say I'm into eBooks myself. I prefer to hold a real book in my hands.'

'Me too.'

Fiona was wondering how she could bring the conversation round to Estelle when Kathleen mentioned the dead woman herself.

'You know one person who knew Jane's work inside out was Estelle.'

'Really?'

'Oh yes. She'd read all the books and could tell you the names of all the characters in them. I think she upset Madison yesterday when she corrected her when someone asked a question.'

'Really? I hadn't appreciated that.'

'Oh yes. You heard her didn't you June?' She turned to June Summerhayes who was helping herself to coffee. 'I was just saying how Estelle upset Madison when she pointed out that it was Mr Knightley not Captain Wentworth who lived in Donwell Abbey as Madison had claimed.'

'Estelle made a very pointed remark about it being a basic mistake that no one who really knew their Jane Austen would make.'

'That does sound harsh.'

'I know one shouldn't speak ill of the dead,' said June, 'but you have to admit the atmosphere is a great deal less tense without everyone having to tiptoe around the woman. Even if she didn't find an excuse to pick a fight with someone, she was accusing all and sundry of moving that blessed handbag of hers so she couldn't find it. She made quite a scene in the garden after we'd been round that little cottage at Chawton.'

'I didn't know about that.'

'Oh yes. But then she did have this habit of upsetting people.'

'Anyone in particular?'

'I think she crossed swords with Renée a couple of times.'

'Do you know what it was about?'

'Renée was making perfectly polite conversation about Estelle reminding her of someone famous, but she couldn't think who. She'd seen a photo in one of the society magazines not long ago. You'd think Renée had insulted her the fuss she made. It was quite embarrassing for the rest of us.'

'I can imagine.'

'She was rude to Imogene as well, but Imogene does strike me as being rather highly strung and quick to take offense,' said Kathleen.

Fiona nodded. 'I agree. I saw them having words in the dining room at Chawton House.'

'That wasn't the first time. On Sunday at the meet-and-greet, Estelle ridiculed something Imogene said. I can't remember what it was about now, but Imogene wasn't even speaking to her, she was talking with her brother,' June added.

Kathleen nodded. 'She did much the same thing to Ruth Lloyd. She's another sensitive soul and prefers not to draw attention to herself. I had a hard job trying to bring her out of her shell when she first joined the book group. Mind you, Erma stepped in and took her to task for upsetting her friend. Gave Estelle a right talking to, told her to pick on someone her own size.'

Fiona looked across at the couple who'd already taken their seats in readiness for the film. 'I don't think I've spoken much to either of them.'

'That doesn't surprise me. They do tend to keep themselves to themselves.'

Any further conversation was cut short when Madison announced that the film was about to start.

Day Four

Jane's health had never been robust, but throughout 1816 it deteriorated considerably. In the New Year, worried by her condition, her family took her to Winchester to consult with Mr Lyford at the County Hospital. His diagnosis was not hopeful. The family took lodgings in the city at Castle Street. Jane's illness, thought today to be Addison's Disease, could not be cured and on Friday 18 July she died with her head resting on her sister's knee. Six days later, Jane was laid to rest in the north aisle of Winchester Cathedral.

After her death, appreciation of Jane's writing grew and in 1870 her nephew Edward wrote a memoir of his aunt.

Our guided walking tour of the city will begin with a visit to the cathedral to see the memorials erected in her memory. Interestingly, the engraving on her gravestone refers only to 'the benevolence of her heart, the sweetness of temperament and the extraordinary endowments of her mind,' and makes no mention of her literary achievements. Several years later, Jane's nephew commissioned a brass plaque on the wall alongside her grave which bears the inscription, 'Jane Austen, known to many by her writings'. The cathedral also boasts a beautiful stained-glass memorial window in her honour.

We will continue to explore this ancient Saxon capital and see No. 8 College Street where Jane spent the last weeks of her life.

Those of you who have seen the 2005 adaptation of Pride and Prejudice *starring Keira Knightly may recognise the locations featured in the film as several of the scenes were shot in Winchester.*

After lunch we leave Winchester and head north to our second hotel via the picturesque village of Lacock. Many period dramas have been filmed here including adaptations of Emma *and* Pride and Prejudice. *There will also be a visit to Lacock Abbey, once home to William Henry Fox Talbot, inventor of the photographic negative.*

We will return to the coach for a short journey to the ancient spa city of Bath, which has attracted visitors since Roman times. Our home for the next three nights is The Spa Hotel just a short stroll from the heart of the city. It was formerly a Georgian mansion set in seven acres of beautiful, landscaped gardens. The hotel boasts excellent facilities with a gym, a large indoor and an outdoor swimming pool and its very own hydrotherapy pool, whirlpool and thermal suite.

Super Sun Executive Travel

Chapter 13

Fiona was still finishing her breakfast when she saw Peter Montgomery-Jones walk through the open door.

'I thought you'd returned to London.'

'You told me if I wanted to speak to your passengers, I would need to get here first thing as you were all leaving for Bath after lunch. I thought while I was waiting, I would come and pester you.'

He gave her a mock-innocent look and took the chair Winston had vacated five minutes earlier.

Her frown disappeared in a burst of laughter.

'Well if you don't mind, I'm going to finish my breakfast first and I don't intend to be rushed. I'm sure they'd rustle you up a cup of coffee if you asked nicely.'

He shook his head. 'I have had sufficient, thank you.'

They talked for a minute or two as she buttered her toast. It was as though the friction of their last encounter had never happened.

'You know, Peter,' she said tentatively, 'It's been preying on my mind ever since you told me Estelle's real identity.'

'Oh.' His expression was wary.

'I can understand why she might have wanted to get away after her husband had been killed in front of her so dramatically. She needed time to deal with the horror of it all on her own as far away as possible from anything that kept bringing it all back to her.'

'If you say so.'

'When Bill died, I felt much the same. The last thing I wanted was everyone fussing around me. Eshe mentioned that she'd had an English governess as a child who talked a great deal about her home country. From the way Madame Barbier spoke of her it was clear this woman meant a great deal to her so I suppose England would have been a natural choice for Madame Barbier to run to.'

'There is a logic to what you say. But I am not sure where this is all going.'

'It doesn't explain why, once she arrived in the country, she promptly booked herself on a holiday tour. It seems totally heartless.'

'Perhaps she hoped the tour would take her mind off her grief.'

Fiona shrugged. 'Possibly. It's certainly not what I would do in the circumstances, but it's not my place to judge. People deal with trauma and grief in different ways.'

She pushed her empty plate away.

'Do you really want to interview my passengers?'

He shook his head. 'Not interview, just an informal conversation.'

'What do you hope to learn?'

'I admit the chances of discovering anything new are slim, but it would be remiss of me not to try.'

'Then I suppose now might be as good a time as any for you to chat with each group as they come down for breakfast. Is there anyone in particular you would like to speak to?'

'I was hoping you might suggest people you think Eshe Barbier may have spent a little more time with than others.'

'She wasn't what you'd call a mixer. She didn't go out of her way to make friends with anyone.'

'Not even Michael Selassie?'

'Especially not Michael. Most of the time, if she wasn't berating him, she either ignored him or treated him like some servant.'

'I see.'

'Now's your chance, Peter. Do you see that couple who have just joined their friends at the large table over by the hot buffet?'

By now the room was getting busy.

'The woman in a pink cardigan with her back to us who

has just sat down and the tall, rather stooped gentleman standing next to her?'

'Yes. That's Kathleen and Anthony Trueman. All six of them at the table are members of the same book club. They usually all have breakfast together. Kathleen probably spoke to Madame Barbier more than anyone else. If I were you, I'd give them a few minutes to get themselves settled and go and join them. I'll need to go and sort myself out when I've finished this anyway. There's always a lot to do the day we leave a hotel.'

It was just before nine o'clock when her phone rang again. Another call from Peter.

'I wanted to let you know that I am about to leave the hotel. Please do not interrupt what you are doing, I rang because I did not want to go without letting you know and also to thank you for your help.'

'Did you manage to speak to them all?'

'I did. The book group kindly pointed out the others to me.'

'That's good. I hope it was useful.'

'Better than I anticipated.'

'Oh?' Did that imply that MI6 had more than a passing interest in the mystery surrounding Estelle's death?

'I will speak to you again this evening, but please, Fiona, remember what I said before. Leave the detective work to the professionals. If this does turn out to be another political assassination, not only could you jeopardise any investigation, you could also be putting yourself in danger.'

The party was due to leave the hotel at nine-thirty. From her previous experience, Fiona was well aware that on checkout days, for a variety of reasons it was rare for the party to leave on time – a factor that was programmed into the timings. Their hotel was on the eastern edge of the city, so the plan was for Winston to drive them all into the city centre to meet their guide at the Visitor Centre.

The skinny six-foot young man who came bounding over to shake Fiona's hand could only be in his early twenties. He introduced himself as Nate.

'We are going to begin our tour with a visit to Winchester Cathedral, one of the largest cathedrals in Europe. If you'd all like to follow me.'

Fiona's initial fears that the enthusiastic guide would set too fast a pace resulting in the slower walkers getting caught up in the town centre crowds proved to be unfounded. Though he had a spring in his step, he stopped every twenty yards and turned back to point out some feature until the backmarkers had time to catch up. Young he might be, but he certainly knew his stuff.

Inside the cathedral they eventually came to the north nave where the group gathered around a black tombstone set into the floor.

'As you can see, her gravestone makes no mention of the fact that Jane was a writer. That didn't come until almost sixty years later in 1872 when her nephew, the Rev. James Edward Austen-Leigh had a memorial brass tablet put up which you can see on the wall over there.'

'He was also the first person to write a biography of Jane,' added Madison, keen to show that she too had done her homework.

'I can't claim to be a Jane Austen expert but,' Nate pulled a collection of rolled up sheets of paper from an inside pocket of his corduroy jacket, 'I've been looking up a few quotes that you might find interesting.'

He unfurled his notes and began to read, 'Cassandra wrote to her niece: "Her dear remains are to be deposited in the cathedral … a building she admired so much." In 1900 she was famous enough for a public subscription to pay for a memorial window. Let's go and take a look at that now.'

The next stop on their tour was the lodging house in College Street where Jane and her sister Cassandra went to stay in the last weeks of her life. Although now a private house, above the door was the blue memorial plaque high on the cream painted walls to mark the place where Jane died in her sister's arms. The house was not far from Winchester College where her young nephews went to school.

As they waited for each couple to stand in the doorway beneath the plaque to have their photos taken, Nate pulled out his notes again.

'I have another quote for you. After she and Cassandra arrived here, Jane wrote to her nephew Edward, "We have a neat little drawing room with a bow-window overlooking Dr Gabell's garden." Dr Gabell was the headmaster at the College.'

~

James Fitzwilliam was surprised to see Montgomery-Jones walk into the outer office.

'I thought you were planning to spend some time up in Winchester, sir.'

'That was the intention, but I believe there was little more to be gained by remaining there.'

James got to his feet and followed the MI6 chief into his office. 'Does the fact that you are back here so soon indicate that Eshe Barbier died of natural causes?'

'The post-mortem suggests a suspicious death. They are still waiting on the toxicology report, but I was assured by the SIO that the case was well in hand.'

'Do you believe him?'

Montgomery-Jones shrugged. 'Difficult to determine. As you might expect, both DS Sanders and his superior were clearly unhappy at my interest in the case. Despite my assurances that I was not there to interfere in their investigation, neither were what you might call cooperative. Were it left to DI Swift, I doubt he would do much more than go through the motions. I may be misjudging the man, but he appears to be leaving all the legwork to his DS. Quite literally. He had a second knee replacement at the beginning of the year but to judge from the crutches propped up against the end of his desk, it would appear he still has difficulty walking. No doubt, his lack of exercise in recent months has added to his weight problems. The man is grossly obese.'

'What about his DS? Do you think he's competent to handle such a potentially sensitive case should it prove to be murder?'

Montgomery-Jones shrugged his shoulders. 'As to that, I have no way of telling. DS Sanders gave every indication he wants to hold on to the case, which is understandable. He is wary of Serious Crime Squad or anyone else taking over. It is evident that DI Swift will be retiring in the very near future on medical grounds if not because of his age. If Sanders can prove himself on this case, it will increase his chances of being considered as the man's replacement.'

Montgomery-Jones removed his jacket and draped it over the back of his chair. 'I need to make a few phone calls. Would you be kind enough to fetch me a coffee and then you can update me on the progress on the Kinyande situation.'

'Certainly, sir.' James turned as he reached the door. 'It's almost one o'clock, would you like something to eat as well? I could get some baguettes from the canteen.'

'Good idea.'

'Any particular filling?'

'You choose.'

Montgomery-Jones was on the phone by the time James returned. Without pausing in his conversation, he indicated that James should take a seat at one of the easy chairs by the large picture window.

The call went on for some time and James sipped his coffee, staring out at the boats making their way down river past the Houses of Parliament. He could just make out the tower of Big Ben. He looked up when Montgomery-Jones came to join him.

'I apologise. The minister does like the sound of his own voice.' Montgomery-Jones lowered himself into the opposite chair and accepted the proffered paper cup.

'I'm afraid there wasn't much choice, sir. Tuna mayonnaise or Coronation chicken?'

Montgomery-Jones wrinkled his nose. 'Either. They probably taste much the same.'

Several minutes later, James finished the last of his roll and screwed up the cellophane wrapper placing it in the now empty cardboard coffee cup.

'So it was a wasted journey.'

'Not entirely. I did take the opportunity to talk to Madame Barbier's fellow passengers which proved interesting but not particularly informative.'

'How did she die?'

'The post-mortem revealed needle marks on her stomach which, according to the pathologist, indicates regular insulin injections.'

'If she was a diabetic, could it have been an accidental overdose?'

Montgomery-Jones shook his head. 'There is also a puncture wound on her shoulder and a second on her buttock. I doubt it would have been physically possible for her to have injected herself. The needle went in here, on her right shoulder blade.' He tapped his own shoulder to indicate and mimed trying to use a syringe.

'And the police have no idea who the culprit might be?'

'If they have, they are not prepared to share their suspicions with me.'

'What about the chap who was with her. Did you speak with him?'

'Michael Selassie. No, I did not get the opportunity. The man had already left the area. I get the distinct impression that the police would dearly like to question him again now they know the cause of death, but despite their efforts they cannot trace him.'

'Surely that's suspicious in itself.'

'Not necessarily. He was the one who reported that Eshe Barbier was missing and the first to be interviewed once her body was found. At that point, he informed the police that the woman was travelling under a false name and identified her as Eshe Barbier, widow of the assassinated president. If it were not for his information, it might have been days before her real identity came to light.'

'Did he have any explanation for her subterfuge?'

'Not really. He appeared to believe that after her husband's assassination, she was concerned for her own safety and fled abroad.'

'If she was trying to keep a low profile, it seems odd that she joined a tour group.'

'Possibly, but given that it would be difficult for her to blend into the background, perhaps she felt safer moving from place to place with a group of people than staying in one location where the arrival of a stranger might provoke more attention.'

'And this Michael Selassie, was he her bodyguard?'

'Apparently not. She travelled alone, but Selassie was concerned about her and managed to track her down to beg her to return to Kinyande. According to what he told Mrs Mason, Eshe Barbier was far from happy when he turned up. Told him point-blank she had no intention of going back and tried to send him packing. I gathered from the other people on the tour, the friction between the two of them was quite open. Though it would seem that Eshe Barbier had something of a reputation for upsetting nearly every one of her fellow passengers.'

'Nonetheless, I'm surprised the police didn't try to prevent him leaving the area.'

'At that point, without an obvious cause of death, it was assumed that she had died of natural causes. There was no reason for the police to detain Selassie any further. With no reason to stay any longer, it would appear that the man returned to the hotel packed his things and checked out first thing yesterday morning. Presumably, he has returned to his own country.'

'Why haven't the police checked the passenger records at the airports?'

'They did. Nothing in that name. Nor is there a record of credit card bills registered in that name anywhere in the country. They did track down the taxi that drove him to Winchester railway station, but he paid in cash. He didn't use a credit card in the hotel either. Paid all his bar bills in cash at the time rather than putting them on his room tab.'

'Which means he was probably using a false name too.'

'That much he admitted to Fiona Mason. He told her that he did not want Eshe Barbier to recognise his name when the tour company sent her the passenger list which is included in the preliminary details a couple of days before the start of the tour.'

'However logical all that sounds, the fact that he cannot now be traced, must make him the prime suspect. Plus the fact that he is the only one who knew her prior to the start of the tour.'

'Be that as it may, finding out who killed Eshe Barbier is not the prime concern of this department at the present moment. The situation in Kinyande is what we need to be concentrating on. Now we have finished eating, perhaps you could update me on the progress that has been made in the last twenty-four hours.'

'Certainly, sir.' James got to his feet, gathered up the paper cups and discarded cellophane wrappers from the small coffee table and made his way to the door. 'I'll collect my notes.'

Chapter 14

The main topic of conversation over lunch was the morning tour and their guide in particular. Nate seemed to have charmed all the ladies in the party.

'Wasn't he splendid?' enthused even the usually retiring Ruth Lloyd. 'It was so thoughtful of him to go out of his way to do all that research on Jane Austen for us.'

'He certainly knew how to ensure he ended up with big tips,' muttered a more cynical Franklin Austin.

His wife gave him a quick dig in the ribs. 'Just because you have no interest in Jane Austen is no excuse for you to be such a grouch.'

Fiona jumped as her phone gave an unexpected buzz. Who on earth could be phoning at this time of day? She didn't recognise the number of the caller.

'Fiona Mason.'

'Ahh. Good afternoon, Mrs Mason. This is DS Sanders. I wonder if you could help me…'

'I'm sorry but it's a little noisy in here, let me just move to a quieter spot.'

There was a door out to a terrace running alongside the room where they were eating.

'My apologies, Detective Sergeant. You were saying?'

'I was wondering if you or any of your passengers happen to have a photograph of Michael Selassie by any chance. I thought he might be included in some of the photos taken earlier in the week?'

'I know I haven't any. I don't usually take photos when I'm working. I'm with the rest of the party now. If you'd like to hold the line for a moment, I'll ask them now. Can you tell me why you want them?'

'Thank you. That would be most kind.'

He hadn't answered her question.

She clutched the phone to her chest and stepped back inside.

'May I have your attention for a moment everyone?'

Only after Franklin had bellowed for quiet was Fiona able to pass on DS Sanders' request.

'Lester might have some. He's been taking lots of the book group in various places to show the club when we get back. I seem to remember him trying to take the whole party when we were outside the Jane Austen House getting ready for our introductory talk,' volunteered Kathleen.

'He's just popped out to the men's room,' said his wife.

Fiona lifted the phone again. 'There is a chance that one person may have one. If he has, I could ask him to email it to you if you'd like.'

'That would be excellent.' He reeled off the address.

'I doubt he'll be able to do that now. It might take a while before he gets a chance to look through them all. It may not be until we get to our hotel.'

'That's not a problem. Though I would be grateful if he could do it today if that's possible.'

'I can't promise that he does, but I will let you know one way or the other this evening.'

'Thank you, Mrs Mason. I appreciate it.'

The drive from Winchester to the little village of Lacock in the north of Wilshire was by far the longest yet. As everyone settled themselves in the coach, Fiona studied the details in her tour manager's notes.

'It says two hours on here, I didn't realise it was that far,' she said to Winston.

'You ought to know by now, the company always overestimate timings to cover holdups, sweetheart. If we go straight up the A34 and join the motorway, we'll be there in an hour and a half easy, or if you want, we could go cross country. It'll add quarter of an hour max. Which do you fancy?'

'If I remember rightly that dual carriageway up to Newbury is as boring as any motorway. Let's take the pretty route through the villages and keep our fingers crossed that we don't get stuck behind too many tractors.'

'Right you are.'

With the exception of the waif thin Imogene, and Fiona herself who had restricted themselves to soup, the others had opted for the substantial main meal of either steak and ale pie, battered cod and chips or a vegetarian lasagne. After the heavy meal, the warmth of the sun streaming in through the windows and the gentle movement of the coach, within ten minutes all her passengers were either asleep or content to stare out at the passing countryside.

Released from any need to keep her charges amused on the journey with a commentary, she slid her notes back into her tote bag and sat back. There were too many thoughts buzzing around in the back of her mind to allow her to doze off herself.

Why was DS Sanders so keen to get hold of a likeness of Michael? Did that imply he was now a suspect in Madame Barbier's murder? Peter may have done his best to persuade her she was jumping to conclusions, but it was obvious that the police were treating her death as suspicious. She may have only had that one real conversation with him, but it had been enough to convince her that Michael was no killer. If anything, the man had seemed panicked at Madame Barbier's absence. As though it had been his job to protect her and he had failed. True he was using a false name, but he had a good explanation for that.

'This pretty little village is one of the oldest in England and it's entirely owned by the National Trust which is why its historic nature has been preserved. You won't see modern buildings or things like telephone cables or anything that indicates we're living in the twenty-first century. Which is why of course, Lacock is such a popular location for all sorts of period dramas. Not only *Pride and Prejudice*, but *Downton*

Abbey, *Cranford* and even scenes in Harry Potter have been filmed here. So, take your time and explore and I'll see you all back here at the coach at five o'clock.'

As her passengers slowly made their way off to stroll through the village, she turned back to the coach and climbed up the steps to collect her things from the front seat. She took her purse from her tote bag and slipped it into her jacket pocket.

'What was that big sigh for, sweetheart? You's been worried ever since you got into the coach. Tell your Uncle Winston.'

She couldn't help smiling. "Uncle" Winston was probably no older than her eldest son.

'You read me too well.' She perched back onto the edge of the seat and looked across at him. 'I had a phone call during lunch from DS Sanders. He wants me to send him all the photos any of the party have taken that show Michael.'

'The chap who left the tour yesterday?'

'That's right.'

'But why do the police want photos of him?'

'That's just it, Winston. The only reason I can think of is that they suspect he murdered Estelle.'

Winston shook his head. 'You sure you's not jumping to conclusions, sweetheart? If it were a proper murder investigation, you'd all have been taken in for questioning.'

'I don't think they realised she'd been murdered until after the post-mortem.'

'So how'd the lady die then?'

'The police aren't saying but I suspect it was an insulin overdose. She was a diabetic.'

'Couldn't it have been accidental?'

'Then why would they be so keen to get hold of Michael?'

Winston shook his head, his broad forehead creased in a frown. 'If it weren't him, you got any ideas who might have done it?'

'Estelle du Plessis had the knack of upsetting almost everyone.'

'But murder! How'd the killer get hold of insulin? I don't suppose it's the sort of stuff you can waltz into the chemists and just ask for. Not without a prescription.'

'No. You're right, Winston.' Fiona thought for a moment. 'Franklin is a diabetic. He may be on insulin injections. I don't know. But that doesn't automatically make him the main suspect. Estelle always carried her injector pen in her bag, and that morning she'd gone back for another phial in case her pen ran out. She made no secret of it. The trouble was, she was forever leaving that bag around and accusing everyone of moving it. I remember someone telling her that was not a sensible thing to do in case she lost her bag altogether and needed her pen. Estelle didn't take kindly to the advice and made another of her scenes.'

'So you're saying any of the rest of 'em could've pinched it.'

'You sound as though you don't believe me.'

'I didn't say that, sweetheart. But perhaps you should have a word with your fellah.'

'My fellow as you call him, would tell me to leave it to the police as well you know, Winston Taylor.'

He gave her a sheepish smile. 'Well, as there ain't nothing you can do about it, it ain't worth worrying about, is it, sweetheart?'

'That wind is quite chilly, isn't it?' said Kathleen pulling the edges of her fleece together as they turned the corner on their way back to the car park.

'It has been much colder today, but it is the end of September. I suppose we should be grateful it hasn't rained,' Fiona replied.

'I suppose so. But what happened to poor Estelle puts a dampener on things. It's surprising how a person can seem hale and hearty one minute and struck down by a stroke or a heart attack the next.'

'Very true. Isn't that cottage pretty.'

'I can't help wondering why it took so long to find her body.' Fiona's attempt to change the subject was ignored. 'It wasn't as if people didn't go looking for her. Michael searched every inch of those grounds. We saw him when we were in the lime avenue. He asked us if we'd seen her.'

'He was very worried.'

'I suppose it was his job to keep an eye on her. Not that she made it easy for him. She didn't have a kind word to say to him from the moment they arrived, but that day…' Kathleen shook her head. 'The poor man obviously had the patience of a saint the way she tore into him. Anyone else would have walked away no matter how much he got paid to be her secretary.'

'I did hear them having words in the walled garden, but I hadn't realised it was that bad.'

'I don't know about that but when they were in the Oak Room, she called him names that I couldn't possibly repeat, and she threatened him. She wasn't shouting and screaming. It was barely above a whisper but that made it ten times worse somehow. I was stuck in that little alcove and I couldn't move out without them seeing me, so I had to wait until Michael stormed off. He didn't say anything to her, but I saw his face as he went past, and I could tell even he was shocked.'

'Did you mention it to DS Sanders?'

'Not the details, I said they had been arguing but he said he already knew that. I wonder if that's what might have caused the heart attack. Something like that can affect your blood pressure. And she was a large lady. I wouldn't call her obese exactly, but she was what you might say well-covered.'

'I don't suppose we'll ever know.'

'I wonder if that's what Michael thought as well. If he thought it was partly his fault he would be upset, wouldn't he? He's quite a sensitive soul, you know.'

'You might be right. I can't say I ever had much of a conversation with him.'

Kathleen gave a sigh. 'I don't suppose anyone else did but me. Even that was only the once.'

'Really?'

'It was that first morning. I'm always an early riser but we'd arranged to have breakfast at eight o'clock with the rest of the book club. Anthony was still asleep, so I decided to go and sit in the gardens at the back. There was a nice little suntrap by the wall with a bench. I was reading my book when Michael came out and we got talking. I remarked on the weather as you do and said it must be a lot hotter back home. We started talking about his country and he said how he grew up in a small farming village but was now living in a big city. He did mention its name, but it didn't mean anything to me. Kin something or other.'

'Kinshasa?'

She shook her head. 'No, I've heard of that. Something with lots of esses. Kinessi? I'm not sure.'

They had almost reached the coach and the conversation was brought to an end.

Chapter 15

The sun had disappeared beneath the horizon by the time they arrived at the hotel on the eastern side of Bath city centre. However, even in the dusk, the approach was imposing. Well-kept lawns and clipped box hedges lined the driveway up to the entrance flanked by Greek pillars and a triangular pediment. If the place was as impressive and upmarket inside, her passengers would have no complaints.

Leaving Winston to help the less agile members of the party down the coach steps, Fiona went inside to check them all in.

She smiled at Lester as she gave him his room key. 'I think you may find it a little more difficult to pop out in the mornings to get your newspaper. I did ask at the desk just now and was told if you let them have the details, they will arrange to have it delivered here for you.'

'That is kind of you, Fiona. I'll do that. And if you give me ten minutes to sort myself out, I'll take a look at my photos and see if I can find any of Michael for the police. I download each day's pictures onto my laptop. It shouldn't take too long.'

'I am so grateful, Lester. No rush. You have my room number.'

Her room was everything she could wish for, including a view over the terraced gardens complete with manicured lawns, geometric flower beds, topiary and even Greek style statuary. It was a pity they had such a full programme, she decided. She could happily spend a good half-day in the hotel.

Lester's call came before she'd finished unpacking her suitcase.

'Shall I meet you downstairs somewhere or would it be easier for you to come to our room and I can show you here?'

'If June doesn't mind, I'm happy to come to you. If your room is anything like mine, there's plenty of space.'

He chuckled. 'They are sumptuous, aren't they?'

It was June who answered Fiona's knock.

Lester was sitting at the small table by the window, his laptop open in front of him. He pulled another chair alongside.

'Hi, Fiona. Come and look at these and see if you think they'll be of any help. Though I still can't see why that policeman wants a photo of Michael. Has he gone missing now or something?'

'I really have no idea. I asked DS Sanders, but in my experience, the police never give much away, do they?'

There was a chuckle from June, now propped up on the pillows, who looked up from the crossword she was working on. 'Had a lot of experience with the police, have you?'

Fiona decided to make a joke of it. 'You'd be surprised at some of the things my passengers get up to. But don't ask, I'm sworn to secrecy.' She really would have to be more careful in what she said. For all her quiet retiring manner, June Summerhayes was clearly as sharp as a chef's knife.

'I think this one is about the best I've got.' Lester was keen to get back to the matter in hand. 'I was trying to get a shot of our group walking back up the steps to the main house. I thought it made a nice picture with the figures in the foreground leading the eye up to the house dominating the upper part of the picture. At the last minute, Michael turned his head and looked back. I remember, I was a bit annoyed when I went through all the photos that evening. Him doing that spoiled the effect of what I was hoping for.'

'I think he was probably looking back to check that Estelle was still there. There she is right at the bottom.'

'Whatever.' From the tone of his voice, it was clear that

Lester was still some way from forgiving the African. 'Anyway, if you blow it up, it's quite a good likeness.'

Fiona leant closer as Lester continued to click on the photos until Michael's face almost filled the screen.

'I've got a couple more group shots to take back to show to the other members of the book club when we get home.'

He clicked through his pictures until he found the ones he wanted to show her. 'I can send him these as well if you like.'

'Great.'

Fiona took out her mobile ready to give him DS Sanders' email address.

'On second thoughts, Piers has already given me one of his, so if you email these to me, I can send them altogether.'

If she had the photos, she could also send copies to Peter.

'Fine. No problem.'

She gave him her email address.

'I have to say Lester, you have some brilliant pictures here.'

'And so they should be, the amount of time and money he spends on his hobby.' There was no rancour in June's voice. It was obvious she was proud of her husband's skill.

As Lester busied himself sending the photos, June gave a deep sigh.

'I give up.' She pushed herself up from her reclining position and dropped her pen on the bedside table. 'I don't know who the paper is getting to compile the crosswords these last few weeks but they're beyond me. I couldn't manage more than half of today's.'

She refolded the paper and threw it on the end of the bed.

Fiona noticed a large picture on the front page – a mob of angry protesters being pushed back by a wall of black-clad forces in full riot gear with transparent shields and clubs. Above it in bold print was the headline "OVER 60 PEOPLE KILLED IN KIDESSI RIOTS'.

It was the name that held Fiona's attention. She'd heard it recently, or at least something very much like it.

Instinctively, she picked it up and read the caption beneath the picture then dropped it back on the bed.

'I'm so sorry. That was very rude of me.'

'It's fine. Take it if you want. Lester's finished reading it and I only bother with headlines unless it's something that particularly interests me. I can't do the crossword, so I was going to chuck it in the bin anyway.'

'If you're sure.'

'Be my guest.'

Chapter 16

There was no time to read the paper when she got back to her room. She needed to finish unpacking her case and then it would be time for a shower and get ready for dinner.

Madison was due to give her last lecture this evening. Although she had assured Fiona that she was happy to go ahead, she had been evasive about its contents. Now she had got to know her fellow travellers a little better, Fiona had to trust that the girl would pitch what she had to say at the appropriate level.

The receptionist had reassured Fiona that a small conference room had been booked for tonight's talk, but she hadn't had time to check it out yet. Madison was proposing to use another PowerPoint presentation, so as well as confirming that the chairs had been set out, there was the question of ensuring the room had the necessary projection facilities.

~

Montgomery-Jones's inner office had been transformed into what now more closely resembled an incident room in a police station. James Fitzwilliam had wheeled in a whiteboard and placed it in front of the large conference table at the far end of the L-shaped room.

James looked up from his laptop. 'That's the last member of Antoine Barbier's inner cabinet, sir.'

Montgomery-Jones replaced the cap on the marker pen and dropped it onto the table before standing back to study the list of names.

'We know that most if not all of them are keen to take over and are jostling for position, but assuming it isn't

Vannier who is trying to destabilise his own control, which of the remaining men do we think is the most likely candidate?'

'According to our man in the Cameroons, General Ademola is the most power hungry.'

Montgomery-Jones perched himself on the edge of the desk looking up at the board and shook his head.

'Possibly. He let the mob overrun great swathes of the city before sending in his troops. But who else might we consider?'

James pushed back his chair and walked round the table. Picking up a contrasting colour marker he put a line through three names.

'From what we can deduce from all the information we've accrued from various sources; I'd say we can rule out these three. They were Barbier's yes-men brought in to do his bidding. Jelani was badly injured in all the initial melee following the assassination itself and is now in hospital and not expected to recover.'

'Toure and Faucher are moderates and Zadzisai and Gowon are both stridently anti-Western. Which leaves us with Xhosa, Ladipo and Timbili. What do we know about them?'

'Neither Xhosa nor Ladipo appear keen to fight for the presidency. Xhosa is happy to support Vannier, Ladipo is General Ademola's man, but Timbili is an unknown quantity.'

'Oh?'

'Despite his lowly office, he was Antoine Barbier's right-hand man. Been with him since they were teenagers. Friends as well as colleagues. Never stepped into the limelight, but always there behind the scenes.'

'None of which has got us far.'

'When all the dust settles, who would the Foreign Office like to see at the top? Do you know, sir?'

'I presume the best option for us would be Faucher, the current Foreign Minister. The new deal was being negotiated with him.'

'And what are his chances, do you think?'

Montgomery-Jones shook his head. 'As things stand right now, I would say slim. Very slim.'

~

'Do you think Madison would mind if we skipped her talk tonight? Renée and I went for an explore earlier and the pool looks fantastic. It's long enough to do some decent lengths. Apart from the fact that we have such a busy programme, at this time of the evening there shouldn't be too many people in there.'

Fiona gave Franklin a beaming smile. 'That is absolutely fine. The talks are entirely optional.'

'We do feel a bit guilty,' said Renée. 'There aren't that many of us left now and we don't want to let her down.'

'You mustn't feel like that. It's your holiday after all.'

The waiter arrived with their desserts. As he attempted to lay the plate in front of him, Franklin put his hand up.

'Not for me. I know I ordered this, but I've changed my mind.'

'Can I get you something else, sir?'

'No, no. If I'm going for a swim this evening best not to do it on a full stomach.'

Franklin and Renée were not the only ones who had decided to skip the lecture. Though the rest of the party had moved straight from the dining room to take coffee in the conference room, neither Ruth nor Erma had arrived by the time it came for everyone to take their seats.

'They sent their apologies. Erma had a headache and as the ladies are sharing a room, Ruth said she fancied an early night anyway.'

As Kathleen bustled away to sit down, Fiona turned to an obviously disgruntled Madison trying to find something consoling to say.

'I was up till gone midnight last night working on this,' Madison said between clenched teeth.

'And I'm sure the people who are here will appreciate it.' She laid a hand on the girl's arm.

Madison stalked to the front, picked up the slide controls and turned to her audience.

'Good evening everyone…'

Though there were few pictures to illustrate her talk, it was clear that she felt passionately about Jane's lack of success as a writer.

'For someone who was so little known in her lifetime, who never joined a literary circle, had no contact with other writers, I'm sure Jane Austen would be surprised at how loved and revered her work has become not only in her own country but all over the world. She would be astonished at the hundreds of films, plays and television productions that have been made of her work. And how those six books, only three of which were published in her lifetime, have proved to be the inspiration for so many films and novels based on those stories including *Bridget Jones's Diary*, *Death Comes to Pemberley* by P.D. James, *Northanger Abbey* by Val McDermid and *Emma: A Modern Retelling* by Alexander McCall Smith.'

The applause that greeted the end of Madison's talk went some way to make up for the diminished size of her audience.

'Congratulations.' Fiona patted her on the shoulder. 'That went down well.'

'Do you think so?' Madison attempted to look modest, but it was obvious she was feeling proud of herself.

More than she deserved to be, in Fiona's estimation, but there was nothing to be gained by saying so. When all was said and done, Madison was still a student with no experience of giving presentations in public.

It was gone ten o'clock before she phoned Peter.

'I can't believe that I was speaking to you at breakfast only this morning. It feels like days ago. Mind you, we have moved hotels.'

'I take it you have been busy.'

'You could say that. But no more disasters, thank goodness.'

'Were you expecting any?'

She laughed. 'No not really. Though to be honest I was worried that Madison's talk tonight might prove something of a calamity. I saw the notes she'd prepared on the evening she arrived, and they were totally unsuitable for our passengers, which I had to point out as tactfully as I could. Not that my comments went down too well at the time.'

'But she took your advice I take it.'

'I don't know about that. It was a bit drawn out and repetitive in places, but it was fine. Not what you might call sparkling. No questions at the end again, which Madison took to mean she had covered everything.' She sighed. 'I'm being unkind. She is young and never done anything like this before.'

She knew better than to ask him anything about why he was interested in the Barbier case or how it was progressing, and they chatted about inconsequential things for a few minutes before she gave a long sigh.

'Oh, Peter. I wish you were here.'

There was a soft laugh at the other end of the line. 'I would dearly love to drop everything and come and join you, but I am afraid there are things I need to keep an eye on here right now.'

She chuckled, 'That is not quite what I meant. It's just that something's happened that's got me thinking and I wanted to talk it over with someone. Nothing really important. Another time, I can tell you're busy. I'll let you get back to work.'

'Fiona, I am never too busy for you.'

'That is nice to know but if you are still in your office at gone eleven o'clock at night, it must be important.'

'How do you know where I am?'

'I know you're not in your study. That grandfather clock

122

of yours has a very distinctive tick.'

'I could be tucked up in bed as I presume you are.'

'I am but I know you can't be. A moment ago, I heard Big Ben striking the hour and that's not possible from your flat. But Vauxhall Cross is only just down the river.'

He laughed. 'How perceptive of you.'

'You are obviously up to your eyes, so I'll leave you to it. I'm not sure what time I'll be able to phone you tomorrow as it's the Regency Ball at the Assembly Rooms…'

'You still have not told me what is on your mind. Has one of your passengers been causing you problems?'

'No. Nothing like that. It's just that DS Sanders rang me. He wanted to know if I or any of the others on the tour had any pictures of Michael.'

'I did hear that the police were having difficulty tracking him down.'

'But why would they want to do that?'

Peter was silent for a moment or two. 'You said yourself, the man hadn't given his real name.'

The hesitation had been long enough to make Fiona suspicious. 'You know something, don't you?'

'I am aware that the police are looking for him. That is all. Why they wish to speak to him again, they have not confided in me.' His voice had lost much of its warmth. He was going all official on her again.

'The only conclusion I can come to is that they must think he murdered Estelle.'

'That is a giant leap even for you, Fiona. Eshe Barbier's death could well be from natural causes.'

'True,' she interrupted before he could start a lecture or warn her off. 'But let's assume for a moment that she was murdered and that the police suspect Michael, I am convinced that he can't have done it.'

'Is that one of your hunches or do you have evidence?'

'Stop being so patronising and humour me for once.'

'Ouch!'

'You didn't see him when she went missing. And before

you tell me he was putting it all on, the reason he was so distraught had nothing to do with him caring about her as a person. It was all to do with whatever had sent him chasing after her in the first place, the reason he needed her to return home.'

'And why was that?'

'I've no idea. When Michael first told me the reason he'd joined the tour was to persuade Madame Barbier to return home, I assumed she'd left her husband and he was being paid by him to get her back. Obviously, that was way off the mark.'

There was a long silence and for a moment she thought he might have ended the call.

'Peter?'

'If Michael did not kill Estelle, then who did?'

'That is why I wanted to talk to you. If Madame Barbier had stayed in the Tapestry Room after the rest of the party had moved on, she would have been noticed by the next group when they came in.'

'Perhaps she was. The police would not have attempted to interview all the visitors that went through the house that day.'

'You weren't there. The guides keep a pretty tight rein on their groups and when the next lot came into the Tapestry Room, their guide would have shooed Madame Barbier on pretty quickly. My lot were being difficult, several petty squabbles and people stomping off, so our girl had a hard job trying to keep them together.'

'Assuming you are correct then it follows that the murderer must be one of your party.'

'Exactly. Estelle managed to upset a great many people in the twenty-four hours she was here. I have been going over and over it but for the life of me I cannot think of anyone who could possibly have a motive.'

'In all honesty I believe you are wrong about this and letting your imagination run away with you. Please Fiona, promise me that you will not do anything rash. You do have a habit of putting yourself in danger and I will not be there…' He stopped short.

'To rescue me,' she finished for him. 'Sometimes, Peter, you can be the most arrogant insufferable man alive.'

She punched the off button.

Day Five

Bath was the place to see and be seen in Jane's lifetime. In the eighteenth and early nineteenth centuries, fashionable society flocked to the city to take the waters, visit the Roman Baths and the fifteenth-century cathedral and admire the beautiful Georgian architecture. Above all they came to enjoy the town's social life, especially its theatre and ballrooms where they could rub shoulders with the well-to-do and the influential. Parents would find husbands for their daughters and suitable wives for their sons.

Jane's mother was born in Bath and the family had strong ties to the city. Jane visited Bath for the first time in 1797 staying with her aunt and uncle. In 1799, her brother Edward came to take the 'cure' accompanied by Jane and their mother, staying in temporary accommodation in the city's fashionable Queen Square. In 1801 her parents decided to move to Bath and Jane and her sister Cassandra went with them. Bath remained her home until her father's death in 1806. It is no surprise to find many references to Bath in Jane's novels especially in Northanger Abbey and Persuasion.

Our first stop will be to the Jane Austen Centre situated in an original Georgian townhouse. Here you will hear the story of Jane's time in Bath, including the effect that living here had on her and her writing from one of the expert guides dressed in period costume. After taking refreshment in the centre's atmospheric Regency Tea Room, we will continue with one of the knowledgeable centre guides on a walking tour, taking us to places mentioned in Jane Austen's letters and her novels, Northanger Abbey and Persuasion. We will see the Bath Assembly Rooms where Catherine

Morland is escorted to a ball, but nobody asks her to dance. The Assembly rooms were used as filming locations for 1986's Northanger Abbey *and 1995's* Persuasion. *We will also pass 4 Sydney Place which was Jane's Bath home.*

One building that Jane would have known well is the Theatre Royal now a Grade II listed building and described as one of the most important examples of theatre architecture. Here we will be taken for a private visit behind the scenes in the company of a long serving member of staff who will tell us something of the building's history.

This evening we will enjoy a special Regency Ball at the famous Assembly Rooms to mark the end of our tour.

Super Sun Executive Travel

Chapter 17

The BBC's early morning Breakfast programme was showing as Fiona was getting dressed. She picked up the controls and switched to ITV's Good Morning Britain, but that was only more of the same collection of general what's-going-on type items. News summaries only happened on the hour and she had a meeting with Winston at breakfast at seven o'clock.

She finished brushing her hair and switched off the television. Perhaps it was worth trying the radio, but it was probably much of the same.

It was almost certainly a waste of time anyway. Disasters happened every day all over the world affecting the lives of hundreds if not thousands of people. They hit the headlines, but the world moves on. The following day they are replaced by some fresh crisis.

Her only interest in what was happening in an African country she'd never even heard of until a few days ago was because of the association with Madame Barbier and Michael. Michael had admitted he'd followed Madame Barbier to persuade her to return to Kinyande, but he wouldn't explain why. Despite all his pleading, it was clear Madame Barbier had no intention of going home. He, on the other hand, seemed equally determined to keep trying. But why? What was so important that he'd travelled all the way to Britain rather than by communicating by phone? From the pictures she'd seen in the newspaper, it had to be the very last place anyone would want to go by choice.

Was Michael back there now? Caught up in what was happening in the capital.

She picked up her notes for the day and headed down to breakfast.

'You sure you don't want me to drive you all to the Jane Austen Centre this morning, sweetheart?'

'Absolutely. It's less than a mile from the hotel. By the time everyone has got in the coach and then got out at the other end, it would have been quicker to walk. Besides, Tom Edwards who normally leads this tour suggested we take a minor diversion to see one of the houses Jane and her family lived in for a short while. Even though it's a private house and we can't go in, from what I've seen of the group so far, they will all want to stop and take photos of the outside. If we leave at nine o'clock, we should arrive in plenty of time to meet the guide for the booked tour. Anthony Trueman is probably the oldest person in the party but despite his stoop and rather vague demeanour, he had no problems in keeping up on our guided walk in Winchester. In fact it was Erma Mahoney and her younger friend Ruth Lloyd I had to keep an eye on, but that was because they kept stopping to look in shop windows, and as far as I can tell, there aren't any on the way to the Jane Austen Centre.'

'In that case, I'll love you and leave you, as they say, and I'll pick you all up again after lunch.'

'Thanks, Winston. I can't afford to sit here much longer either. As soon as the centre opens, I need to ring to confirm the timing of our visit and the number of people they can expect.'

~

Peter Montgomery-Jones looked up as James knocked and came in holding a piece of paper.

'Have they managed to establish when Eshe Barbier entered the country?'

'Yes, sir. She arrived at Heathrow on the fifth of September on a flight from Schiphol.'

'Which would appear to confirm what she told Mrs Mason.'

'She used a Kinyande passport in her own name, but we

have not been able to trace her movements since. If she booked into a hotel, she used a false name. Either that or she went to a pre-arranged safehouse. Though as far as we can tell, she had no known friends in this country. We found no trace of an Eshe Barbier or Estelle du Plessis before she turned up in Winchester.'

'What about the man calling himself Michael Selassie?'

'Without his real name, it's proving considerably more difficult to track him down. Because of all the troubles, the numbers of people fleeing the country has meant extra charter flights not only from Kinyande but the adjacent countries. Trying to track passenger lists leaving the area has been chaotic to say the least. We have collated details of all males of the appropriate age with Kinyande passports arriving at British airports and ferry terminals. It's running into hundreds already, but he could easily have flown anywhere in Europe and made his way here by private plane or boat. I've sent the photo of Selassie you received from Mrs Mason last evening to the research department and they've started the process of checking it against passport photos of those on the list. They said not to expect results any time soon as all they had were names and passport numbers.'

'What about Kinyande citizens travelling to Kindessi in the last two days?'

James shook his head. 'Only a handful, but we're still checking all Kinyande nationals departing to countries with direct flights to Kinyande.'

The Jane Austen Centre occupied a three-storey house nestled in the centre of what had been one of Georgian Bath's fashionable terraces, facing onto the park in Queen Square. They were greeted at the door by an imposing gentleman with long bushy side whiskers, dressed in black tailcoat, large white cravat and beige breeches.

He tipped his top hat and pointing to the life size mannequin dressed in blue coat and black bonnet said, 'On behalf of Miss Jane Austen herself, may I welcome you to the centre.'

All the staff inside were dressed in period costume, including the enthusiastic young woman who was to lead them through the various rooms who introduced herself as Georgiana Darcy.

She took them first along a corridor lined with portraits of Jane and all her family and information boards about Jane's life and times.

After their tour, nearly everyone bought something from the shop, from books to Jane Austen themed jewellery, mugs and tea towels. Fiona spotted an illustrated volume of Jane's letters with a pretty floral cover which she decided would make a suitable thank you gift for Madison at the end of the tour.

The Centre's Regency Café was buzzing with excited chatter. Even the men in the group seemed to have enjoyed their morning so far.

'What did you enjoy most?' Fiona asked June Summerhayes as she picked up her teacup.

'Everything was wonderful, but it was fun trying on costumes, especially the bonnets.'

'I think all the women loved doing that. I'm not so sure about the men, but I did notice that Renée even persuaded Franklin to dress up.'

'I think all the men tried on at least a wig or hat, except Lester. He claimed he was too busy taking everyone's photo.'

'Poor Anthony didn't look very comfortable being made to have a photo taken in his frockcoat, but Piers was in his element strutting about like a real Regency dandy. Mind you he has the figure and the hair to go with it.'

June laughed. 'I think Imogene had a job getting him to take all that clobber off and put his own jacket back on at the end.'

It was time to think about going round the tables to remind everyone they would all be meeting their guide for the walking tour of the city in five minutes. Fiona noticed an earnest conversation going on at one of the tables. The three women were all leaning forward, their heads only a foot or so from each other.

'Is anything wrong?'

They all looked up at Fiona looking a trifle sheepish, but no one replied.

Eventually, Kathleen said tentatively, 'There's a rumour going round that Estelle was murdered and that the police have arrested Michael. It's not true is it?'

'My goodness. Where on earth did you hear that?'

Ruth Lloyd dropped her gaze to her lap.

'Ruth overheard Madison talking with Piers and Imogene.'

'I'm sure you must have misheard. I am a hundred percent certain that if that were the case, I would have been told.'

Even if DS Sanders may not have informed her about Michael's arrest, she was certain Peter would have warned her. For all his insistence on keeping his work and social life completely separate, the news would have leaked out eventually and Peter would have let her prepare her remaining passengers in advance of any media revelation.

The figure standing alongside the model of Jane Austen to the right of the entrance steps was so still that Fiona didn't notice her at first. She was dressed in a short, bust-length, close-fitting crimson jacket above a long white skirt and a bonnet of the same crimson velvet tied under her chin with a broad white ribbon. The high stiff brim was lined in a pleated white fabric which framed fair curls that fell in two long ringlets almost to her shoulders.

As the last of her party were emerging from inside, Fiona went over to introduce herself.

'You must be our guide for the Bath walk. I'm Fiona

Mason, the tour manager.'

The young woman tucked the two books she was holding under her left elbow and held out her hand. 'Elizabeth Bennet. Pleased to meet you.'

'Are all you centre guides named after Jane Austen characters?' asked Imogene who had overheard the conversation.

'We are.'

When everyone was gathered round, Elizabeth Bennet led them to a suitable spot where they would not obstruct passers-by.

'In *Northanger Abbey*, Catherine Morland says, "Who can ever be tired of Bath?" and today I am going to prove to you just how true that statement is.'

She held up copies of two of Jane Austen's books.

'The location for both *Northanger Abbey* and *Persuasion* is this beautiful city. On our walk this morning I'm going to show you some of the places associated with Jane and her books. Jane lived in Bath for five years from 1801 and 1806 together with her parents and her sister, Cassandra...'

No one was getting left behind as they ambled slowly south in the direction of Bath Abbey, but Fiona was concerned that Anthony might be having problems.

'I was wondering if you might be having any difficulty hearing our guide. I appreciate with all the noise of passing traffic and everything else going on it's not the same as in the peaceful gardens where we've been before.'

'I'm fine, my dear. She has a lovely clear voice and though I admit I don't catch every word it really isn't a problem.'

And you probably wouldn't tell me even if you hadn't heard any of it, she thought. If only all her passengers were more like him. A good old-fashioned gentleman who never caused any bother.

They passed the imposing Bath Abbey with its magnificent stained-glass windows a short distance from their first stop which was the Pump Room.

'Here in this building, Catherine Morland is first introduced into society. It's the centre of much of the action in *Northanger Abbey*. You can almost feel Jane herself observing people parading through the room to find inspiration for her colourful characters.'

Their pretty young guide's enthusiasm had them all smiling as she promenaded up and down in front of them bowing to left and right as though she were Jane Austen herself acknowledging acquaintances.

'As you see, next door to the Pump Room are the famous Roman Baths. In Jane's day, the baths themselves were open to the public and although it's true that Jane never mentions the Roman Baths in any novels, it is more than probable that she joined her high society friends for whom taking a dip in these mineral waters was all part of the Bath experience.'

Despite the fact that they had all been on their feet for well over an hour, everyone seemed disappointed when their tour came to an end and they had to say goodbye to their lively young guide.

~

Reports of the coup were coming in thick and fast.

'General Ademola's troops stormed the Presidential Palace, Vannier was arrested and Kindessi is now under military control,' James reported.

'Any news on what has happened to the rest of the cabinet?'

'No, sir. Nothing definite, but it looks as though all of Vannier's supporters are being rounded up plus the remaining pro-Western liberals. Ladipo and a couple of the other hardliners have declared support for Ademola, but the picture is still very confused. It doesn't look good for any of our people still out there.'

Montgomery-Jones shook his head. 'The Foreign Office is doing everything it can, as are our people in neighbouring countries.'

James gave a sigh. 'The chances of ever finding our missing man are getting slimmer by the hour.'

Chapter 18

It was no good. She couldn't put it off any longer.

'Madison, may I have a word?'

The rest of the party made their way into the restaurant for lunch.

'Let's step outside for a moment.'

This was the first opportunity to speak to the girl where their conversation could not be overheard.

'I hear that there are stories going around that Michael has been arrested for the murder of Estelle du Plessis.'

Madison's eyes widened. 'Really!'

'You sound surprised.'

'I am.'

'But aren't you the one who told Imogene that Estelle was murdered?'

'That's not true. The pair of us were talking about why the police came back to question us all again.' When she saw the look on Fiona's face, she became defensive. 'I may have said something like anyone might think Estelle had been murdered the way we were interrogated.'

'And then you went on to speculate that Michael had been arrested for killing her.'

'It wasn't like that.' Madison shook her head vigorously. 'I just said it was strange that the police contacted you after we'd moved on to ask for pictures of Michael.'

'The point being Madison, as I have told you before, you do not get involved in any kind of gossip with the passengers. It can lead to all sorts of problems and in this particular case it has. Your conversation was overheard and like all Chinese whispers it has quickly escalated out of proportion.'

Madison looked crestfallen, opening and closing her lips,

clearly unable to think of what to say.

'You have placed me in a difficult position. I now have to go in there and undo all the damage you have done. By rights, I should make you apologise for being the source of false rumours.'

'I'm sorry. I didn't think...'

'That is my point Madison. You didn't think. You are not a passenger on this tour. You are here in an official position as a guest lecturer. You signed a contract which stated that you would do and say nothing that would either bring the company into disrepute or upset the passengers.'

There were loud sniffs and Madison pulled a handkerchief from her pocket.

'One more thing, I appreciate that you have become friends with Imogene, but from now on I think it best if you refrain from spending so much time with her. Remain polite obviously but you need to maintain your distance. No more girlie chats. You are here to look after all the group, not just one person. Do you understand?'

Madison's lips tightened, but she gave a perfunctory nod.

'I suggest you go to the cloakroom and wash your face before you go back in there.'

~

There was a buzz on the intercom. 'Jean-Claude Durand on the line for you, sir.'

'Put him through, James.' Montgomery-Jones pressed the button for the outside line. 'Jean-Claude, what can I do for you?'

'It is more what I can do for you, Peter. Your missing trade delegate turned up at the French Embassy in Kindessi late last night.'

'That is good to know. Any chance of your people getting him out of Kinyande for us?'

There was a chuckle at the far end of the line. 'If I can arrange for him to join some of our French nationals on the flight into Morocco, you will have to take it from there. I will send you the details when the arrangements are finalised.'

'I am very grateful. I owe you one.'

'Indeed, you do.'

~

It was a very chastened Madison who returned to join the rest of the party at lunch. With only twelve places at the long table, she had no choice but to take the empty chair beside Fiona who was no doubt the last person she would have chosen to sit next to. If any of the others noticed how subdued Madison was, none of them remarked on it. Most were too busy extolling the qualities of Elizabeth Bennet and her presentation.

'Wasn't she delightful?' said Ruth.

'And so knowledgeable. I never realised that of all the places where Jane stayed, only 4 Sydney Place has a plaque to show that she lived there,' added June Summerhayes. 'Lester has some really good pictures of us all standing underneath it, don't you, dear?'

'They look alright, but we'll have to wait until I can load them up on my laptop and see them all on a decent sized screen. It's difficult to tell with group shots. There's always someone with their eyes closed. That's why I like to take several.'

'You'll have to take all our emails and you can send us all copies,' said Franklin.

They had just finished lunch when Fiona received a call on her mobile.

'I expect that will be Winston asking what time to bring the coach round. Forgive me everyone while I go somewhere a little quieter.'

She glanced at the number as she hurried outside. She knew it couldn't be Winston as he always waited for her call, but she didn't recognise the caller's number. Please don't let it be the police again.

'Hello,' she said tentatively.

'Is that Fiona Mason?'

'It is.'

'Fiona, this is Michael Selassie. I am sorry to trouble you, but I do not know who else to call.'

'Michael! The police are looking for you.'

'I know.'

'Where are you?'

He seemed reluctant to answer her. 'Not far. Can we meet to talk somewhere? Just the two of us.'

'I am in Bath right now. We're about to go into the Theatre Royal.'

'Things are getting out of hand. I need your help. I do not know who else to ask.'

'Our backstage visit shouldn't take much more than an hour or so and then we'll be returning to the hotel. It's the Regency Ball at the Assembly Rooms this evening and the costume hire people are meeting us there at five o'clock for everyone to choose an outfit. I could perhaps meet you then.'

There was a long silence.

'Are you still there, Michael.'

'Yes.'

'Can you tell me what this is all about?'

'Is it true that Estelle's death was not... Was she murdered?'

'I really don't know. All I can tell you is that the police have been asking a lot more questions. They also wanted copies of any pictures that include you.'

'They think I murdered her, don't they?'

'I honestly don't know, Michael.'

'I swear to you that I did not. Her death is the worst thing that could happen.'

'I don't understand.'

'Whoever killed her, is going to kill me.'

'What are you talking about? Who could possibly want

you dead?'

'I don't know who exactly. An assassin sent by someone senior in my country.'

'Michael, I don't know how you think I can help. You need to go to DS Sanders and explain it all to him.'

'No.'

'If it would help, I'll come with you.'

'No. It would not help.'

There was a long silence. She wasn't sure if he'd ended the call.

'I am sorry. I should not have bothered you.'

'Wait, Michael. Please don't ring off. Listen, once everyone is in the theatre and the tour is underway, I'll try and slip away. If you could come to the café, there is an entrance from the street and it's open to the public not just theatregoers, I'll meet you in there.'

'What time?'

'Say three o'clock. Would that be possible?'

'I will find it.'

'It's called the Egg Café. You can't miss it.'

Quite why she had arranged to meet him she wasn't sure. What possible help she could give him she had no idea, but the man had sounded so desperate. She couldn't just ignore him.

Chapter 19

'The architect who built this theatre also built the notorious Newgate Prison in London in 1770…'

After their guide, an elderly gentleman who had obviously trodden the boards himself in his younger days, had finished his potted history of the theatre, he led the way out of the foyer.

'Madison, a word.'

She heard the girl mutter, 'What now,' under her breath.

Madison turned and threw Fiona a poisonous look.

Fiona let the rest of the party troop past in the wake of the guide into the main auditorium.

'I have to slip away for five minutes and I need you to look after the group while I'm gone. Do you think you can manage that?'

The girl gave an exaggerated sigh. 'I suppose so.'

'There is no suppose about it. Unless you stop sulking and stop behaving like some hard done by adolescent, you are for the high jump, young lady. Is that understood? I've put up with your nonsense for far too long.'

Madison looked suitably chastened.

'Okay.'

'Good. I'll be back as soon as I can.'

Michael was sitting in a dark corner, a cup of coffee in front of him, his eyes focused on the street entrance. His face was drawn, and he looked shrunken from the tall imposing figure she had last seen. He was smartly dressed, and it was clear wherever he had been for the last three days, he had not been sleeping rough.

She slipped into the seat next to him.

'I cannot stop long. I should be next door with the group.

You said before that you were both travelling under false names. I now know Estelle was the widow of the assassinated president and I take it you are also from Kinyande.'

'My name is Mosi Timbili.'

'That doesn't mean anything to me, I'm afraid.'

'I am… was a junior minister in Antoine Barbier's government. Antoine and I grew up together in the same village. We were close. Like brothers. I did not agree with many of his more recent policies, but I still supported him.'

'Were you also a close friend of Estelle?'

He shook his head. 'I believe Eshe resented our friendship. Since his marriage, Antoine and I had grown more distant. Eshe and I were always polite to one another but never what you might call friends. That is why I used a false name. I knew she would never agree to see me if I tried to approach her openly.'

'I still don't understand why you followed her all this way?'

'How much do you know about what is going on in my country?'

'Not a great deal. Obviously, the assassination was reported in all our media and I know there are riots going on now. There are pictures in the newspapers and on TV showing the clashes between the protesters and the military and whole areas of the capital going up in flames.'

'The prospects for our future are not good. Those in charge of the government are divided. The Acting President is not strong enough to pull them together. The hardliners are opposed to the pro-Western sympathies of the moderates but even they are not united. There are competing factions determined to take the country in different directions with the military on one side and the Marxists on the other. I came to persuade Eshe to come home and take control. She was our best hope. She was the only one who could still command the respect of both Antoine's people and the hardliners such as General Ademola and Gowon.'

'But she refused, I take it.'

He nodded.

'Why didn't you say all this to DS Sanders?'

'I told him her real name so that her body could be returned to her own country. I did not want her buried over here as a stranger. At the time, I assumed Eshe had died of natural causes and there was no need to give him more details. He was happy to let me leave which is why I returned to the hotel to collect my belongings and head back home. There was no reason for me to stay. Next thing I knew the police were looking for me. I do not understand. Why did they let me go if they thought I was responsible for her death?'

'I don't think the police appreciated that her death was suspicious until the post-mortem had been conducted, which wasn't until the following day. I am sure if you explained all this to DS Sanders…'

'I am not going to the police. I would be arrested straight away. You said they wanted my picture. They would not understand. They have no other suspects.'

'Have you any idea of who did kill Madame Barbier?'

'It could only be one of my people. I have no evidence to prove an assassin was sent to prevent her return to my country. Even if they were prepared to consider my story, how could they even begin to find evidence?'

'Where have you been?'

'DS Sanders took me to the mortuary on Monday night to identify Eshe's body, then he and an Inspector Swift asked me a few more questions. The Inspector appeared to think the case was closed and said that I was free to go. I was driven back to the hotel. Next morning, I checked out and caught a train to London. There were no suitable flights that day, so I booked into a hotel using my own name. That night I had a phone call from my wife back in Kinyande warning me not to go back. While I had been gone, the situation back home had worsened. All of Antoine's supporters in the government had been put under house arrest or had

143

mysteriously disappeared. Police had come to our house that afternoon demanding to know where I was.'

'I don't understand how I can help.'

He gave a long sigh. 'I am not sure you can, but there is no one else I can ask. If there is an order out for my arrest in Kinyande, I have nowhere to go. If I go to the British police I will be arrested. I thought that if you could put my story to the authorities, they might listen to you.'

'There is one person I could talk to, but it may not be easy to get him to act on your behalf.'

'I have no other option.'

'I will phone him now but if I stand any chance of persuading him, I will need to speak to him face to face. I can't leave Bath, but he may be prepared to come down from London. Once I've had a chance to explain everything, I will ring you.'

He blinked rapidly to hold back his tears. 'Thank you, Fiona.'

'I cannot promise he will agree to help.' The last thing she needed was to raise his expectations.'

'I appreciate that.'

She glanced at her watch. She'd been gone much longer than she'd intended.

Fiona was surprised to see Imogene standing in the foyer when she went back into the theatre.

'Is anything wrong? Why aren't you with the others?'

'I had a headache and it's a bit claustrophobic in the dressing rooms.'

'I'm sorry to hear that. Is there anything I can get for you? Some water perhaps, I can go…'

'Don't bother.'

Imogene didn't look unwell. If anything from the way she was glowering at her, she looked if not exactly annoyed then belligerent and resentful.

'What is the problem, Imogene?'

'Why did you tell Madison that she couldn't speak to me

144

anymore?'

'That is not what I said. I simply reminded her of her duties as the guest lecturer was to see to the needs of all the passengers.'

'It was pretty mean to say you would make sure she was fired if you caught her talking to me again. I've a good mind to report you to Super Sun.'

'That is your right of course. Though for the record, I made no such threat.'

Imogene took a step towards her, her fist raised.

The door to the back of the theatre suddenly opened and Piers raced in.

'Imogene!'

Imogene spun round to face him.

'There you are!' he continued in a soothing voice. 'I looked around and you were gone.'

'I came to get some air.'

'Come on, Sis. You're missing all the good bits.'

He put his arm around her and gently ushered her back the way he'd come. As he reached the door, he looked over his shoulder, a pleading expression on his face.

'Thanks for looking after her, Fiona. I'm afraid my little sister does tend to become a little overemotional on occasions. She'll be fine in a tick.'

Fiona was about to follow the couple backstage when she realised she still hadn't phoned Peter. That little scene had almost wiped it from her mind.

Her call was answered after two rings.

'Fiona, what can I do for you?'

'I need to speak to you urgently. Are you busy right now?'

'I am as it happens. Why? What has happened?'

'Not over the phone. I appreciate it's a big ask but is it possible for you to come down here? It's just too complicated to explain over the phone. I wouldn't ask but it is important.'

There was a long pause.

'Please, Peter. I wouldn't ask, but you're the only one who can help.'

'Can you at least give me an idea of what it is about?'

'It's to do with Michael.'

'What about him?'

'I've just been speaking to him. He said he didn't kill Madame Barbier and I believe him.'

'Then I would suggest you persuade him that his best course of action is to go to the police and tell them.'

'He feels they won't believe him, and he will be arrested.'

'This is Britain. It is not a police state. He cannot be charged if there is no evidence against him.'

'I think you should talk to him first. His real name is Mosi Timbili.'

There was a long pause. 'If I leave now, I should be there by six-thirty.'

'That will be fine. I'll give you the hotel postcode.'

The name had meant nothing to her, but to judge from the sudden change in his reaction, it was clearly significant to Peter.

Chapter 20

The costume hire people had already arrived at the hotel by the time the party arrived back from the theatre. Racks of dresses were being unloaded from a van parked close to a side door ready to be wheeled through to the large conference rooms set aside for them. Then came two large wicker baskets which Fiona presumed contained wigs, fans, gloves and other such paraphernalia.

'Just to remind you, you can go down and choose your costumes any time after five-thirty. There is no need for you all to rush down there at once. You have until seven o'clock so there is plenty of time. As you can see there will be plenty of choice so no one will miss out if you choose to go for a swim first or make use of any other of the hotel facilities. I know some of you have already booked sessions in the spa area. Finally, the coach will be leaving for the Assembly Rooms at a quarter to eight so please be down in the foyer dressed in all your finery five minutes beforehand.'

She put out a hand to help Kathleen down the steep coach steps.

'Seeing all those gorgeous costumes has made me feel quite excited. I'm really looking forward to the evening.'

'It promises to be a great occasion,' Fiona replied.

'Though whether I'll still have enough energy left to remain on my feet by then is another matter,' she added when the older couple were out of earshot.

There was a low chuckle from inside the coach. 'As bad as that, sweetheart?'

'You wouldn't believe, Winston. There are days when I wonder why on earth I do this job and today has been one of them.'

'You love it all really.'

As the coach drew away, Fiona shook her head. 'I'm beginning to wonder. Perhaps it's time to call it a day.'

Too tired to tackle the stairs, she took the easy option and pressed the lift button. In her room, she dumped her bag on the chair, shrugged out of her jacket, kicked off her shoes and collapsed onto the bed, lay back and closed her eyes.

There were things she ought to be doing but right now she was going to take a ten-minute break. Just empty her mind and lie there. Perhaps she should sign up for one of those meditation classes being advertised in the local paper when she got home. Learn to shut out the world and recharge her batteries.

She woke with a start.

Time to rouse herself. The cup of tea would have to wait. She needed to check that all was well with the costume people before her passengers arrived to make their choices. At least that ten-minute nap had done the trick. She felt a great deal livelier than when she'd laid down.

There was no problem finding the correct room. A big notice "Super Sun Costumes" had been put up outside. She put a head round the door. There was a mature woman who Fiona assumed to be the manager, arranging wigs on a stand with the help of a much younger woman, plus a young man kneeling on the floor beside a large wicker hamper.

'Do you have everything you need?'

The woman turned and smiled.

'I'm Fiona Mason, the tour manager.'

'Oh yes, you're Tom's replacement. I was sorry to hear about poor Tom. How is he?'

'As far as I know he wasn't hurt in the accident. It's his wife who is still recovering. I take it you know Tom.'

'Oh yes. We've been providing costumes for the Regency Ball for several years now. Let me show you how we organise everything. First people will select their outfits and then the ladies can try them out in that room and the men in the room to the left.'

'I noticed the no entry signs on the doors when I came down the corridor.'

'If they need any help getting into them, Simone and Andrew can give them a hand. We start packing away all the spares at seven o'clock, but we'll hang around till half past in case anyone's having a problem getting into their outfits – arranging wigs, tying cravats and the like.'

'That's very good of you.'

'Would you like to choose your costume now?'

'Oh no. I'll let my passengers make their choices first. You did get my message that there will only be ten of them now plus two staff, did you?'

'I did, thank you. Four gentlemen and eight ladies.'

'In that case, I'll leave you to it.'

'Please pass on my good wishes to Tom and say I hope his wife recovers soon.'

'I will.'

There were only a few people in the café. Fiona noticed Ruth Lloyd and Erma Mahoney sitting at a window table. Luckily, they hadn't spotted her so she was able to find a table on the other side of the room before they could invite her to join them. She needed to work out exactly how to approach the thorny problem of Michael with Peter. Getting him to help was by no means a foregone conclusion. She would need to choose her words carefully without putting his back up.

It would help if she knew exactly how Madame Barbier had been killed. Though she'd convinced herself it was the result of an insulin injection, perhaps she should review the evidence again. Obviously, Madame Barbier hadn't been shot or stabbed. The police would have noticed and realised she had been murdered as soon as her body had been discovered. By the same logic, presumably she couldn't have been strangled as the evidence would have been easy to spot. Fiona didn't know enough about poisons to be able to rule that out, but if something had been slipped into her food or drink at lunch time, it might explain why the killer didn't need to be physically present in the Tapestry Room at Chawton House. One of her political opponents could have doctored the food though it was difficult to see how.

The killer could not guarantee that Madame Barbier

would not collapse in front of anyone else but perhaps that did not matter. Fiona shook her head. That idea wouldn't work. Her body had been hidden behind the screen. The killer had to be physically present.

How else was it possible to murder someone without any obvious signs? Could she have been injected with a fast-acting poison?

It was only after Fiona had left the café that it occurred to her that perhaps she shouldn't leave it too late to collect her costume. If Peter was going to be here at six-thirty she didn't want to have to dart out in the middle of their conversation.

Fiona picked a relatively modest outfit for the ball. A simple grey silky affair with enough lace around the neckline to cover any cleavage. Nothing that would draw attention.

She hung up the dress on the back of the wardrobe and had just finished laying out the rest of the outfit – bonnet, shoes, gloves and reticule – in readiness, when her phone rang.

'My goodness. Did you break the speed limit getting here so quickly? It's only just gone quarter past.'

'I was lucky with the traffic. No holdups.'

'I'll come down now.'

They found a quiet corner in the lounge. Fiona made sure that she sat directly facing him. Peter Montgomery-Jones might be the master of the deadpan expression, but she needed to be able to detect the merest flicker of reaction in his face or the way he held his body.

'First and foremost, Peter, I've asked you here as a friend. I need your advice.'

'I hope I am always that.' The shutters were coming down already.

'I appreciate your position and that never under any circumstances would you say or do anything either directly or indirectly that would compromise your role or breech any confidence under the Official Secrets Act or whatever it's called. Nor would I expect you to. I very much doubt that anything I have to say touches on anything that affects the security of this country. But, as it is concerned with the death of Eshe Barbier, it does relate to the politics of a foreign country.'

'Go on.' He sat back in the easy chair and crossed his legs, resting his elbows on the arms of the chair in an open gesture.

'Do you know exactly how Madame Barbier died?'

'As I told you before, that is a matter for the police, and I am not involved in the case.'

'Which I take it means that you do, but beyond that Her Majesty's Security Services is not involved. However, I doubt that the powers that be are too happy with the repercussions that might ensue when the news that such a significant political figure has been murdered on British soil hits the headlines should it prove to be the case.'

He raised an eyebrow and smiled ruefully.

'I am going to make the assumption that Madame Barbier was killed by a lethal injection. Probably a massive overdose of insulin.'

He laughed. 'And you reached this conclusion – how?'

'Logical deduction. Because her death was assumed at first to be from natural causes there could have been no obvious signs of violence, but because an attempt to hide her body from immediate detection, whoever killed her had to be physically present at the moment of her death.'

'I cannot fault that logic.'

'Given that the police appear to be conducting an all-out search for Michael Selassie and that there have been no further attempts to interrogate any of my other passengers, it is safe to assume that Mosi Timbili, as I suppose I should now call him, is the main suspect.'

'I have no knowledge of how the police are conducting the case or what conclusions they have drawn so far, but I can only agree with you and assume that the situation is as you have just described it.'

He was back to official-speak but there was no point in losing his sympathy by pointing it out.

'I appreciate that the police are aware of Estelle's real name and the fact that she was the widow of the late President of Kinyande, but I doubt they appreciate Michael's true identity.'

'About that.' Peter's face remained expressionless, but she could sense he was less than happy with her. 'I am interested to know why you have not mentioned his real name until now.'

'I've only just found it out myself when I was speaking to him.'

His eyebrows shot up.

'When was that?'

'About three hours ago. Just before I phoned you.'

'You know where he is?'

'Not exactly.'

'And what is his story?'

'It might be better if he told you himself.'

'You said you did not know where he was.'

'I don't. But I do have his phone number.'

He shook his head in exasperation.

It felt good to turn the master's tricks back on himself.

'Before you speak to him and listen to what he has to say, I need your assurance that you will hear him out and not hand him straight over to the police.'

There was a long pause.

'How can I answer that until I am satisfied that he poses no threat.'

'Point taken. Let me tell you what he told me.'

Chapter 21

Once she had contacted Mosi, she handed her phone to Peter.

'My name is Peter Montgomery-Jones. I am a member of Her Majesty's Security Service. Mrs Mason has given me an outline of your situation. I am prepared to talk with you and if I am happy with the answers to all my questions, I believe I am in a position to help. It may be possible to offer you temporary political asylum here in Britain until the position in your country becomes clearer, if that is what you would like.'

Fiona could not hear Mosi's reply, but she assumed he had agreed to Peter's terms.

'In which case, if you would like to suggest a meeting place, I will join you now.'

Peter ended the call and returned Fiona's phone.

'He agreed to meet on condition that you accompany me.'

She glanced at her watch. 'I have to be back at half past seven at the latest. We are leaving the hotel at seven forty-five and I have to change into my ball outfit.'

'He insisted we meet out in the open. He proposed Sydney Gardens.'

'That's a ten-minute walk from here. Even less if we cut through the grounds at the back of the hotel.'

Mosi was sitting on the grass in the centre of a large open area watching two small boys playing cricket with their father some distance away. He got to his feet as he spotted their approach.

'He does not trust you, Peter. He wants to make sure that if you have warned the police, he is somewhere he will be able to see them coming.'

'I would not have expected anything else.'

As they got nearer, Peter held out his hand. 'Peter Montgomery-Jones and you are Mr Mosi Timbili, I presume. There is a bench over by the lake, shall we go and make ourselves more comfortable.'

The big African looked around suspiciously, but the bench was well away from any cover that might conceal any followers. He nodded.

'Fiona has told you my name. How much do you know about my country?'

'Sufficient to be able to appreciate the power struggle that is going on. Mrs Mason said that you told her that you came to this country to persuade Madame du Plessis, or to use her real name, Eshe Barbier, to return to your country. Was that statement correct?'

Mosi frowned. 'It was. My objective was to make her appreciate that without her, the ONP would disintegrate into warring factions and the government would collapse.'

They had reached the bench.

'But if as you told Mrs Mason, you and Madame Barbier were never on good terms with one another, what made you think you could succeed? Surely that fact rather suggests the opposite. You came expressly to prevent her from returning.'

'No.' Mosi clenched his fists. 'The decision for me to be the one to come was not mine. Paul Faucher sent me.'

'The Foreign Minister?'

'Yes. He feared that he and the other senior liberal ministers were being too closely observed by General Ademola's men. Any of them would be stopped before they reached the border.'

This time, it was Peter's turn to frown. 'Enlighten me, Mr Timbili, here in the West, Antoine Barbier was never perceived as a liberal.'

Mosi smiled. 'He wasn't and neither was Eshe. He was a law unto himself. He leaned one way on some issues and then the other. Whatever suited him at the time. He was no angel. But he had control. He managed to assert himself in a party that included both right- and left-wing elements. His was a powerful personality that he used to manipulate people, bribing them off to keep the lid on the simmering pot. That was the point. Now he is gone. The pot hasn't just boiled over, it's exploded. Whatever happens now, we will all be the losers, those in power and the vast masses in the countryside. There will be no winners.'

The sound of a lone bird singing its heart out was the only thing that broke the heavy silence that had descended.

Eventually, Peter said, 'If as you say you did not kill Eshe Barbier, who did?'

'Presumably one of General Ademola's men. Someone in whose interests it was to prevent Eshe from returning to Kinyande. I can only assume that my departure from Kinyande was noted, and I was followed in the hope of leading them to Eshe. That is why I need help now. My life is in danger. Whoever murdered Eshe will want to kill me to prevent me telling what I know to the authorities. But as things now stand, if I attempt to go to the police, my story will not be believed, and I will be charged with her murder.'

'Has any attempt been made on your life in the last two days?'

'No not yet. I have managed to evade them, but I cannot do so for much longer.'

'Forgive me for interrupting, but may I make a point?'

Both men turned and stared at Fiona.

'I accept what you have just been saying, but I'm not convinced that Madame Barbier was murdered by someone from your country. Her body was found hidden behind a screen in the Tapestry Room. Therefore, whoever killed her had to be in that room to move her body to delay it being found. So how did your man from Kinyande or an assassin hired by one of your countrymen get into the building? Any stranger not part of the group would have been spotted immediately.'

Mosi's expression hardened. 'You are saying I killed

155

Eshe.'

'No. You don't have to convince me, Mosi. I believe you. What I am saying is that I am far from persuaded that this was a political murder. The only other people who could have killed her had to be members of our party and they would have to have a totally personal reason to take revenge on the woman they knew only as Estelle du Plessis.'

'But who?'

'I wish I knew. I have absolutely no idea. You know as well as I do, Madame Barbier appeared to delight in upsetting as many people as possible and as often as she could, but enough to kill? It has to be more than that.'

'I have to agree with Mrs Mason.' Peter nodded. 'I need you to think, is there anything else that might help us to apprehend the killer?'

Mosi frowned looking confused. 'I have never considered the possibility…'

'This evening is the last event of the tour. Tomorrow morning all my passengers will be leaving and making their way home. Estelle's murderer will be free to make their escape unless the police are informed and take action.'

'What are you saying? You are asking me to turn myself in.'

'They have to know, Mosi.' She put a hand on his arm. 'You cannot be responsible for letting a killer go scot-free.'

Mosi shook his head.

'This is not a police state, Mr Timbili,' said Peter. 'You cannot be charged without evidence. In fact, I can see no case for detaining you. I am happy to accompany you to the police station. Though I am not a lawyer, my position does give me some authority. I can see no alternative. You cannot evade the police indefinitely. The longer this situation drags on, the more difficult it will be to explain why you did not come forward earlier.'

Mosi hung his head. Eventually, he looked up and turned to Peter then nodded.

Peter took out his phone. 'I will ring the ministry and ask

them to begin steps to grant you diplomatic immunity.'

Fiona glanced at her watch. 'I need to be getting back to the hotel. If you would both excuse me, gentleman. Good luck, Mosi. You are doing the right thing and you are in the best of hands.'

Chapter 22

Fiona raced up to her room. There wasn't really time for a shower, but she was hot and sticky, she'd have to make time.

Thankfully, the simple dress she had chosen had no complicated fastenings and the bonnet would hide her hair. No time for elaborate makeup, she would have to make do with a touch of lipstick and a dab of powder on her nose.

She was by no means the first to arrive in the lobby.

'My goodness, don't you look magnificent. I hope Lester has already taken several photos of you to show your family when you get home.'

June Summerhayes raised her fan to cover the lower part of her face and giggled. 'He has. I took a couple of shots of him as well.'

Fiona turned to Lester looking quite distinguished in the high collar and snowy white lace at his throat.

'Let me have your camera and I'll take one of you both together.'

Everyone else was doing much the same.

Fiona had to raise her voice to quieten the excited chatter and it took Franklin's bellow to get their attention.

'Is everyone here now?'

With all the wigs and top hats, Fiona found it impossible to count.

'The coach is here so if you would like to make your way on board, ladies and gentlemen, let's go to the ball.'

She hurried to hold open the door not so much to allow the ladies to lift their skirts to step outside but to count that she had all ten passengers plus Madison.

Though Madison had hung back, keeping well away from Imogene in compliance with Fiona's instruction, Fiona did not miss the defiant look the girl threw in her direction as she skipped through the door. The gown she had chosen was almost identical to that which Imogene was wearing. Madison's was a pale pink and Imogene's of the exact same cut but in a soft mauve. Their wigs, gloves and fans were identical. It was evident that the women had dressed as sisters. Their choice of costume had clearly been prearranged but both were all too well aware that Fiona would never be able to prove it.

Fiona laughed. She had far more important things to occupy her mind than concern herself with childish tricks.

Madison glanced back over her shoulder. The surprise at Fiona's reaction had wiped the gloating look from the girl's face.

It took some time for everyone to get onto the coach. Holding up their long skirts up the narrow steps and central aisle was no easy task. There were enough spare seats for the ladies not to have to crush their petticoats by sitting alongside their usual partners.

'Are we all settled?' Winston called from the front.

'I can't fasten my seat belt,' came a wail from the back.

As Fiona went to unbuckle hers, Winston put out a hand. 'Leave it to me, sweetheart.'

Tonight, was the first time that Fiona had no concerns that her guests were not enjoying themselves to the full. Even the normally self-effacing Ruth and Erma who generally preferred to take a back seat were fully entering into the lively spirit of the place. Their rosy cheeks glowed with pleasure as two young men came to invite them on to the dance floor to be guided through a few simple stately steps of a couple of sedate Regency dances.

Only Fiona felt unable to enjoy the festivities. Her mind was on other things. Until she knew that Peter had managed to arrange for Mosi to be given asylum, she could not be sure that DS Sanders would not arrest Mosi the moment he clapped eyes on him without stopping to listen to Mosi's story of events.

There was nothing she could do to help for the next few hours so there was no reason for her not to enter into the joyous spirit of the evening. No matter how many times she tried telling herself that fact, her concern for Mosi overrode everything else.

The call came late in the evening. It took several moments to extract her mobile from the silly little reticule that matched her gown. A glance at the caller number indicated that it was not from Peter but DS Sanders.

'What time do you anticipate you and your party will be returning to the hotel?' Straight to business. He was not one for pleasantries.

'Good evening to you too, Detective Sergeant.' The sarcasm was probably wasted on him. 'The ball ends at eleven o'clock. I would imagine it will be a further half hour before we get back.'

'Good. I will be there.'

Without waiting for her response, he cut the call. He was obviously not in the best of moods. His opportunity to arrest his prime suspect had been taken from him. The case had been blown wide open and he and his team were back to square one. Imagining how the purist Peter Montgomery-Jones would wrinkle his nose at the collection of clichés now running through her mind made her smile. Not that the current situation was amusing. Not in the slightest. Life was going to get a great deal tougher.

DS Sanders stepped from the front doors of the hotel even before Winston had a chance to bring the coach to a stop.

The door swished open and he mounted the steps. He picked up the microphone and turned to face everyone.

'Ladies and Gentlemen. I apologise for troubling you all at this hour of the evening, but I am compelled to have to give you some distressing news. We can now confirm that the death of your fellow passenger Estelle du Plessis was in fact murder.'

160

Excited chatter broke out behind her and Fiona caught the words, 'told you so,' though who had said it she was not sure.

'Quiet please, everyone. I have to tell you that no one will be allowed to check out of the hotel until they have been interviewed.'

'Then why don't you find that secretary of hers and arrest him instead of bothering the rest of us? He's the obvious suspect,' demanded an irate Franklin.

'Exactly...'

Everyone began calling out.

'Quiet!' the DS's voice boomed in the enclosed space and the protests subsided to a muted muttering.

'As I was saying. Everyone will be interviewed...'

'But it's almost midnight.' Even Ruth had been roused to protest.

'Interviews will take place tomorrow morning. Please make yourselves available from nine o'clock onwards.'

'You have no right to detain us without grounds,' protested Lester Summerhayes. 'You have no power to stop us collecting our things and leaving the hotel right now.'

'No one is going to be interviewed under caution, but I would remind you, ladies and gentlemen that this is a murder enquiry and you are all material witnesses to the events that led up to the final moments before Mrs du Plessis's death.'

'But...'

'That will be all, ladies and gentlemen.' He thrust the microphone into Fiona's hand and stomped down the steps only to have to pause to wait for Winston to press the button to reopen the door.

'What a beastly end to what has been the most magical day of the whole holiday.' Even the ever-patient Kathleen who never had a critical word to say against anyone, was moved to vent her frustration.

Fiona waited until the noisy outbursts had calmed down before gently tapping the microphone for attention.

'It is getting very late, everyone. May I suggest you all

make your way to bed. We will learn nothing more tonight so as Kathleen has just pointed out, it has been a fantastic day so don't let this announcement ruin it. Sleep well everyone and do your best to put this unpleasant business out of mind.'

Whether she could do the same, she very much doubted.

Once she'd helped everyone down the coach steps, Fiona said goodnight to Winston and made her way into the hotel. Preoccupied with her own thoughts, she hadn't noticed DS Sanders waiting by the reception desk until she heard her name being called out.

She turned towards him doing her best to disguise her irritation.

'Sergeant?'

'A quick word.' He led her away from the desk, his eyes dancing around to ensure their conversation could not be overheard. His expression was grim. 'I understand that you are aware of the true identity of Michael Selassie.'

'I am, but before you accuse me of not informing you earlier, I only learnt that fact a few hours ago. I urged him to speak to you.'

'So I understand, but what I need to know is are your passengers aware of who he and the woman they knew as Madame du Plessis really are?'

'Not as far as I'm aware and certainly not from me.'

'Good. Please don't inform them until after the killer is apprehended.'

'Detective Sergeant, believe me the least said about the whole affair, the happier both I and Super Sun Executive Travel will be.'

'One last thing, do you by any chance have a copy of the home addresses of the members of your party?'

'I'm afraid not. Only their emergency contact details. The company Head Office would be able to let you have a copy.'

'I appreciate that,' he said irritably. 'I would have preferred not to have to wait until morning.'

He turned and started to walk back to the two uniformed officers still waiting by the desk.

'Sergeant. Before you go, may I just ask, was Madame Barbier's bag with her when her body was found?'

The expression on his face suddenly changed. 'Why do you want to know?'

'It's just that I have been giving a great deal of thought to Madame Barbier's last movements and I am fairly certain that I saw it over her shoulder as we left the main hall but I don't remember seeing it after that.'

He gave a deep frown. 'Tell me, Mrs Mason, why do you believe the whereabouts of Eshe Barbier's handbag is of any significance?'

'If it was missing, I thought it might be important. She always carried her medication around with her, but she was very lax about putting her bag down and forgetting where she'd left it whenever we were out on a trip. I just thought you should know.'

'I still cannot see why you think that I should be made aware of that fact.'

Fiona sighed. 'Because if Madame Barbier was murdered with an overdose of insulin there is a good chance that the killer took it from her bag some time earlier.'

His eyes narrowed, he took hold of her elbow and all but frogmarched her across the lobby to one of the café tables.

Chapter 23

He waved her to a chair and sat opposite.

Without preamble he said, 'You are making a big assumption about the cause of death.'

'Possibly, but I'm not wrong, am I?'

He stared back at her, his expression revealing nothing.

'Eshe Barbier died of an overdose of insulin and it was not self-administered,' she continued. 'You appear to have already decided that Mosi is the culprit. All I wanted to do was to point out other people had an opportunity to get hold of her medication.'

They glared at each other for a full half-minute.

'I appreciate you consider yourself something of a detective…'

'That is not true.'

He held up a hand. 'I urge you to leave the detective work to the professionals. Let me make myself very clear, Mrs Mason. Contrary to what you might believe, neither I nor my team have been so determined to prove that Timbili murdered Madame Barbier that we have not investigated other suspects on the Super Sun tour including you.'

'All I'm asking, Detective Sergeant has the bag been found?'

'Are you suggesting that someone stole her bag?'

'Not necessarily. She was always putting it down and forgetting where she'd left it. Someone might easily have seen it lying around and taken the medication from it.'

'For the time being, let's go with your theory. Who else would know that she was a diabetic?'

'Everyone. It wasn't a secret. She made a big thing of it on our first evening together.'

'Are you seriously suggesting that someone just happened

to spot her handbag lying around and decided on impulse to steal her insulin and stab her with it when the party reached the tapestry room?'

Choosing to ignore his attempt to ridicule her, Fiona leant forward folded her arms on the table and stared straight at him holding his attention.

'No, Detective Sergeant. Madame Barbier was clearly unwell when we entered the house. The overdose was given a great deal earlier. I believe it happened in the garden probably when she was alone with her killer. Madame Barbier was complaining that she'd been stung by a wasp. She was rubbing the back of her shoulder. Plus, I think if anyone had stabbed her with a needle so high on her body someone would have noticed. It might just be possible to jab a needle into the top of someone's leg or bottom in a crowded room, but you certainly couldn't raise an arm that high without being spotted. Plus, she would have made a fuss.'

'Perhaps everyone had moved on and the two of them were alone.'

'No, it couldn't have happened like that. The effect of an insulin overdose is not immediate. It would have taken some time for the drug to take effect. I noticed she looked dizzy and confused when we first came into the house, but when I went over to ask if she wanted to go back to the coach, she brushed me off. She was a proud woman who didn't like to appear vulnerable. Then later, there was a scene when Imogene Carnegie claimed that Madame Barbier had pushed her out of the way. With the benefit of hindsight, I think that in her disorientated state, Madame Barbier accidently stumbled against Imogene but was too proud to admit that she was unwell. By then her speech was getting a little slurred. Not badly but several of the others thought she was drunk. Which is why they all steered clear of her.'

'Timbili claims that she was killed by a political rival... someone from his country, which if she was killed in the garden...'

Fiona shook her head vigorously. 'The fatal injection may have been administered outside but whoever killed her had to have followed her into the house because after she collapsed her body…'

'…was hidden behind the screen. Yes, Mrs Mason. We had worked that out. We are called detectives for a reason.'

She grinned. 'I'm sorry.'

The ice was broken. He smiled back.

'What I was about to say was that she was a big woman. Once she'd collapsed, it would need a strong man to drag her up those steps into that position, which of course still leaves Mr Timbili as a suspect.'

'Possibly, but when I last saw her, she was at the far end of the room studying the map. If she felt faint, perhaps she sat down on the steps and then collapsed backwards. Even a woman, assuming she was determined enough, could have rolled her legs up those three or four steps and pulled the small screen in front to hide the body temporarily.'

He stroked his chin. 'Possible, I suppose.'

'If only I could remember who was still in the tapestry room with her when I left. I was convinced she was feeling unwell, but after her response earlier I didn't want to provoke a scene by checking up on her for a second time. Two or three other people were still there, so knowing she wouldn't be left on her own, I moved to the next room.'

'You sure you can't recall who?'

She closed her eyes, put her hands over her face and tried to picture the scene.

'As I said, Madame Barbier was at the far end of the room and there was another couple bent down tracing a route along the streets near the bottom of the London map. The woman laughed. It might have been Renée and Franklin Austin, but I can't swear to it. There was someone else on the other side of the stairs reading one of the information boards. A woman I think, but I didn't really look at any of them.'

She saw him jot down the names.

'Though I'm not sure that really means anything.'

He looked up. 'What are you saying?'

'The next two rooms were devoted to the exhibition. The walls were covered with information boards and display cases. We were all given quite a bit of time in there and people were spread out and moving back and forth. Anyone in the group could have nipped back into the tapestry room without being noticed.'

'I see.'

'Whoever did kill Madame Barbier, Sergeant, must have planned all this in detail. It wasn't done on impulse.'

'Exactly.'

She frowned. 'But who could have had a motive to do it? They had only known her for less than twenty-four hours.'

'Except for Mr Timbili.'

'Except for Mosi.'

Day Six

Today marks the end of our adventures in the Footsteps of Jane Austen and this morning is your opportunity to explore this beautiful city on your own. There is much to see including the Roman Baths and the famous Sally Lunn's Eating House and Museum. Sally Lunn's buns – a rich teacake made with cream and eggs – were so famous that even Jane wrote about them to her sister.

You might choose one of Jane's favourite walks and take a stroll along the Royal Crescent enjoying the views over the park. Here you can also explore No. 1 The Royal Crescent, the most complete Georgian House in Bath.

Another possibility for your consideration is a visit to Bath Abbey, a former Benedictine monastery founded in the 7th century.

Our goodbye lunch in our hotel is a last chance to say a fond farewell to your fellow guests. Once you have checked out of the hotel, the coach will leave for London and independent travellers are free to make their own arrangements.

All of us here at Super Sun hope you have had a pleasant holiday and wish you a safe journey back home. We look forward to seeing you again in the not too distant future, if not on another of our Footsteps tours then travelling with us a little further afield on one of our European tours on the continent.

Super Sun Executive Travel

Chapter 24

Winston looked up as Fiona came in for breakfast. His smile quickly turned to a look of concern.

'You don't look you's usual perky self this morning, sweetheart. You not get a lotta sleep last night?' He poured tea into a clean cup and pushed it across the table in front of her.

'Not a lot, I have to admit. I was talking with DS Sanders until almost one o'clock in the morning.' She lifted the cup and took a slow sip.

'I thought he said the interviews was this morning.'

'They are. The police are coming back. Estelle was definitely given an overdose of insulin. I think they still suspect Mos...Michael. But things have moved on a lot since then.' She explained about her contact with the man he knew only as Michael on the previous day and how Peter had become involved.

'But then ain't it likely that one of these African activists followed them both and that he's the one what did it?'

'It's difficult to see how anyone could have got in Chawton House who wasn't booked on a tour. And DS Sanders' announcement that he and his team are coming this morning to interview everyone would suggest they don't believe it was an outsider either.'

'You sayin' they think one of our lot must've done it?'

'Exactly. But it's possible that they didn't intend to kill her, just make her so ill that she'd have a fit and have to leave the tour. I can think of several people who would be glad to see the back of her. Young Madison for one.'

They sat in silence drinking tea and deep in thought.

Fiona eventually broke the silence. 'Imogene is highly emotional. Verging on unbalanced at times, and she and

Estelle were always at loggerheads. I can imagine her lashing out in the heat of the moment, but whoever killed Estelle put a considerable amount of planning into the deed. I can't see Imogene capable of cold-bloodedly devising a plan to send Estelle into a diabetic coma. There again, it's impossible to appreciate what people are capable of, especially when you've known them so short a time.'

'She went too far, you think?'

Fiona shook her head. 'But that doesn't explain why she would hide the body after she'd injected her. If only I could remember where everyone was that day. One thing I do know is that after the row they'd had in the garden earlier, Michael was keeping his distance from Estelle. I do recall he left the Tapestry Room long before me and I didn't see him again until I went into the second exhibition room. That's why I'm convinced he is not the murderer.'

Fiona lingered over breakfast for some time. She had no need to rush and no deadline to meet. She sat observing her passengers as each small group came into the room and headed for their customary places. First down as usual were Ruth and Erma who gravitated to one of the larger tables not far from the hot buffet. They were joined not long after by a very bleary-eyed Lester and June Summerhayes who both looked as though they were suffering from an overindulgence from the night before.

Fiona sat staring at each of them in turn. Although Madame Barbier had passed a few uncalled-for derogatory remarks aimed at Erma in particular, Erma had been feisty enough to snap back. Fiona couldn't remember any specific incidents when Madame Barbier had picked a fight with any other of the book group. Beside which, she found it impossible to imagine what plausible motive they could have to kill the African woman.

It was a good ten minutes later that Piers and Imogene put in an appearance. From the giggling and excited chatter between them it was impossible to imagine that either of them had murder on their minds and obviously had no concerns about the impending police interviews.

A wary-looking Madison stood in the doorway her eyes scanning the room. Fiona smiled but the girl gave no response. Either she hadn't seen her or chosen to ignore her. Probably the latter. Not that Fiona was put out. She did however catch Imogene's eye and the older woman beckoned Madison to join them.

Madison had been the first to fall foul of the formidable Madame Barbier on the very first evening and she had continued to smart ever since. Madame Barbier had not just ridiculed her ignorance, just as Madison was flushed with success after her first lecture, she had been toppled from the pedestal. Made to look foolish in front of what she saw as her admiring audience. The girl had not shown a jot of regret when she'd heard about the woman's death, but that still did not make her a murderer.

It was no good. She couldn't sit here indefinitely and all this going over things wasn't getting her anywhere. Time to go.

Kathleen came bustling in just as Fiona reached the door. Anthony stood back to let Fiona pass. If he'd been wearing a hat, he would have raised it in greeting. A real gent, was Anthony. They were both such polite, friendly, normal people it wasn't even worth considering them as suspects. Particularly as they were among the few Madame Barbier had never picked a fight with.

'Do you know if the police are here yet?' Kathleen asked.

'I was just on my way to the reception desk to find out.'

Anthony shook his head. 'Dreadful business. Simply dreadful.'

She didn't notice him at first. The movement in her peripheral vision caught her attention as she crossed the lobby on her way to the reception desk. He continued to fold the newspaper he'd been reading and stood up. She made her way over to where he'd been sitting.

'Peter. I hadn't appreciated you were coming. Are you going to be in on the police interviews?'

He raised an eyebrow. 'I think that is the last thing our DS Sanders would allow. He is none too happy at my insistence at being present should he wish to interview Mosi Timbili, but as things stand at the moment, the police investigation into the murder lies outside my jurisdiction.'

Fiona laughed. 'Then why are you here?'

'To see you.' He gestured for her to take the easy chair beside him and they both sat down. 'I thought you might be curious as to how things went last evening.'

'I'm dying to know. You don't know how difficult it was for me to stop myself from ringing you last night. The only reason I didn't was because I realised how busy you must be trying to sort everything out. Once DS Sanders announced when we arrived back last evening that he intended to interview us all again this morning, I assumed that you had managed to prevent him arresting Mosi.'

'For the time being at least. However, DI Swift has made it clear that Mosi Timbili remains his prime suspect.'

'DI Swift?'

'He is heading the investigation.'

'I've never ever seen the man. But do go on.'

'Last night he made it clear that the only reason he has arranged to interview other possible suspects is because this morning is the last opportunity before your tour party leaves the district. How thorough those interviews will be remains to be seen.'

'Does that mean Mosi is still in custody?'

'No. They have his passport and all his details and are no doubt taking steps to ensure he doesn't slip out of the country.'

'How is he?'

'Exhausted I would imagine. I left him in his hotel attempting to get some sleep. It was a particularly fraught night to put it mildly. Convincing DI Swift and his team to consider other lines of enquiry was no easy matter. Not to mention attempting to obtain the minimum of signed documentation to establish Mr Timbili's status at that time of the evening demanded cashing in a good number of favours on my part.'

'You must be pretty exhausted yourself.' Though he had shaved, she realised he was still wearing the same suit and tie as last evening – something she could never remember happening before. The man had more ties than she had dresses in her wardrobe at home. To the best of her knowledge, she had never even seen him in the same suit two days running.

'I assume you haven't been to bed. Shouldn't you be getting some rest yourself?'

'There is still too much to do. I need to return to London, I have other important matters to attend to, which is partly why I am here, to let you know.'

She frowned. 'But are you in a fit state to drive?'

He chuckled. 'Perfectly. I snatched a couple of hours sleep just before dawn.'

There was so much more she wanted to ask. So much more she wanted to say. But not now. He had an important job to do and it would be wrong to detain him further.

They walked side by side to the entrance doors. He bent and kissed her cheek as he said goodbye.

She watched his car drive away until it turned out of sight. Feeling very alone she turned. What had she been going to do before he came? She took a deep breath and walked towards the reception desk.

Chapter 25

Because it was a short tour involving only four full days, Fiona had plenty of room in her suitcase. She'd added a couple more outfits and an extra pair of shoes. There was no point in taking extra reading matter. There was less than the usual amount of down time for passengers on this trip, and she always had arrangements to check and paperwork to complete for Super Sun. Nonetheless, at the last minute, she'd decided to pack her laptop.

Inevitably, it still lay in the bottom of her case where it had been since she'd left Guildford. Now, with time on her hands, would be a good opportunity to do a little research on the internet.

It took her a few minutes to find the details from the slip of paper in the small folder holding her room key card and sort out the login and password details. Technology was not her strong point and she had to make three stabs at it before she got it right.

A week ago, she'd not even heard of Kinyande. Even now she knew next to nothing about the troubled country. Most of the items that came up were current news reports about the demonstrations, protests and riots going on in the last few days. That wasn't what she was looking for. There didn't even appear to be much on the country's past.

She tried a few entries which gave a brief account of the history of Central Africa as a whole. She skipped the sections on early settlement and prehistory. That whole Equatorial area appeared to be a melting pot of tribal conflict as waves of people moved in from north, south, east, and west long before the arrival of European explorers.

During the last two decades of the nineteenth century, Belgium, France, Great Britain, and Germany competed for control of Equatorial Africa. The various boundary lines created between the territories claimed by the invaders in the name of their respective nations took no account of tribal boundaries. Kinyande had become a French colony.

Fiona skimmed the sections on the exploitation of rubber, ivory and timber and the later concessions given over to colonial entrepreneurs for timber extraction, rubber, palm oil and cotton plantations and largescale farming.

The main impact the discovery of the vast mineral wealth of the whole area came later but the latter half of the twentieth century saw a halt to the colonial period. Once the black nationalists of West Africa had won the right to self-determination from Britain, the other countries had little choice but to follow.

Kinyande remained a colony for much longer than the surrounding countries but eventually French colonialism gave way to independence in the early 1970s. Not that it did much for the majority of its people other than provide them with a purely temporary boost in morale at being free from European rule. Foreign companies still controlled the mining industries and without the money for the investment in machinery and the necessary management skills, much of the farmland returned to the people soon reverted to natural scrub.

There were two or three interesting articles about the dramatic changes in the economy over the almost forty years of independence. She was halfway through one outlining the changing political picture and the various freedom movements since the late 70s which again appeared to do little for the impoverished masses, when the bedside phone broke the silence.

'You asked to be informed when the police arrived, Mrs Mason.'

'Thank you. I'll be down straight away.'

Closing the lid of her laptop to automatically put the machine into sleep mode, she found her shoes, and headed for the door. She wanted to catch DS Sanders before he began his interviews.

DS Sanders was standing at the hotel entrance holding open the door for a grossly overweight man struggling up the steps on crutches. At first, she thought he was simply being polite to a new guest but once the fat man was inside the lobby, the policeman fell into step beside the newcomer.

Fiona caught the detective's eye. He beckoned her over.

'Guv, this is Mrs Mason, the tour manager for the group.'

Whether the man's purple face and sour expression was the result of his recent exertions or his annoyance at meeting her, she wasn't sure.

The small, piggy eyes glared at her as he barked, 'So you're the blasted woman whose been interfering with my investigation!'

'*Your* investigation?'

DS Sanders hastily intervened. 'This is Detective Inspector Swift, he is leading the...'

Interrupting his junior, the DI raised a crutch jabbing it at Fiona, 'I want a word with you, missy. If it were not for you muddying the waters, this case would be all sewn up and we'd have our man locked up in custody.'

He continued to shout at her for a good two minutes.

Fiona glared at him biting back the comment that charging an innocent man was hardly justice.

The tirade went on until the DI was out of breath and needed to sit down. As he collapsed onto a nearby sofa, Fiona turned to leave.

'Come back here. I haven't finished with you yet.'

'Perhaps we could speak to Mrs Mason somewhere a little more private,' intervened DS Sanders. 'The hotel has set aside a couple of suitable rooms for the morning's interviews.'

Ten minutes later, Fiona found herself sitting behind a table facing the two detectives with a third much younger officer at the far end poised ready to make notes. The inspector was still wheezing and kept shifting his weight, trying to get comfortable on the chair that was much too small for his bulk.

'I understand that when you last spoke to my Sergeant here, you asked if Eshe Barbier's handbag had been found.'

'That is correct.'

'Exactly why was that?'

'As I explained at the time, because Madame Barbier always carried around her medication with her and was in the habit of leaving her bag around. Anyone could have spotted it and used the opportunity to take out her insulin.'

'Is that the real reason?'

'I don't understand.'

'I have to tell you that this morning we recovered it from the lost property box at Chawton Hall.'

'Where was it found?'

When he gave no reply, DS Sanders answered.

'Tucked behind the curtain at the end of one of the padded window seats in the dining room.'

'Did they think it had been deliberately hidden?'

'No way of telling. It was tucked right at the end, but Madame Barbier could have sat on the window seat and forgotten about it.'

'Can we get on?' Obviously annoyed at his junior's intervention, the inspector snapped his fingers at the constable. 'Hand me my briefcase.'

Once it was placed in front of him, he clicked open the catches and took out a piece of paper protected in a clear plastic sleeve and placed it in front of Fiona. 'Have you seen this before?'

She studied it carefully, frowning at the words. 'Yes. No.'

'Which is it?'

'I mean I haven't seen this particular note, but I received an identical one on our first morning. Exactly the same words and written on a similar piece of paper torn from a ring notebook.'

'Really?' The inspector raised his eyebrows theatrically.

His sergeant continued with the questioning but without his boss's accusing tone. 'What did you do with it?'

'I screwed it up and threw it in the waste bin.'

'So you no longer have it?'

She shook her head.

'Do you know who sent it?'

When she hesitated, the inspector snapped, 'Well?'

'I had a suspicion at the time, but if… Where did you find this?'

Both men answered at the same time.

'We are the ones asking the questions.'

'In Madame Barbier's handbag.'

'It can't be the same one because, as I said, I screwed mine in a tight ball so I could toss it into the bin, and this has no creases.' She slid the plastic sleeve back across the table.

'A likely story,' snapped the inspector. 'Admit it, you were the one who put it there.'

Even the sergeant looked at him with raised eyebrows.

'I suggest you test it for fingerprints.' She glared back at the inspector, but it was DS Sanders who replied.

'We will, but as I'm sure you are aware, that takes time which we don't have right now.'

Fiona frowned. 'I'm surprised Madame Barbier never mentioned the note. I'd have expected her to have made a great fuss and demand I find the culprit.'

'I doubt she ever found it,' said DS Sanders. 'The envelope was still sealed. We have no way of telling exactly when it was put there. If as you say, she frequently left her bag lying around, it could have been slipped in at any time.'

'I suppose so.'

'Tell us about your note. How was it delivered?'

'It was left for me at the front desk in the hotel.'

'And you chose to ignore it?' Even the sergeant looked sceptical.

'Yes. At the time, I thought I knew who'd sent it.'

When she didn't elaborate, the inspector leant forward.

'For pity's sake woman, who did you think it was?'

She was reluctant to tell him.

He slapped a hand on the desk, making everyone jump. 'Mrs Mason, may I remind you this is a murder investigation.'

'Exactly. The point is, I may have been wrong. More than that, knowing what I know now, I am certain that I jumped to the wrong conclusion on Monday morning. I've no wish to prejudice your investigation and send you in the wrong direction.'

'Let us decide what is and what is not relevant. When you first read the note, who did you think had sent it?'

She took a long breath. 'Madison Clark.'

'Why?'

'Several reasons. Madison and I didn't exactly meet on the best of terms. At the last minute, the previous tour manager had to be replaced. As I'm not a Jane Austen expert, the company approached the head of the English department at Winchester University to arrange for one of his students to accompany the tour. However, Madison had been given the impression that she was taking over from the tour manager and that she was in charge of the group. Our first meeting didn't exactly go well, and I fully admit that it was partly my fault. I was tired after a long journey and I didn't handle it well. Later that evening, there was a scene. Madison was rude to one of the passengers and I had to read her the riot act and she stormed off. When I went up to her room to speak to her, she had worked herself up into a state and through the door, I could hear her shouting and she used those exact words; "mean, vindictive bitch! It's all her fault." At the time, I decided the best thing to do was to leave her to cool down and speak to her in the morning.'

'Did you tackle her about the note?' asked the Sergeant.

Fiona shook her head. 'I didn't find the note until the evening by which time Madison seemed to have calmed down. She'd apologised to Madame Barbier and done her best to ingratiate herself with me and kept well away from

Madame Barbier. I thought it best to ignore the note which she could have written in anger and regretted afterwards. To be honest, I put her attempts to impress me by her exemplary behaviour all day down to her feelings of guilt about writing it.'

'If the note was left at the reception desk, why didn't you ask who'd left it?'

'I did. The girl wasn't sure, but she thought it may have been a youth in a baseball cap. I did wonder if what I'd heard the previous evening outside Madison's room was a phone call between her and her boyfriend and he was the one who actually wrote the note. As I said, I never bothered to find out.'

'We will need to speak to Miss Clark.'

Fiona frowned. 'But, in hindsight, I honestly don't think she was responsible.'

'It shouldn't be too difficult to find out if she had a notebook like the one these pages were torn from,' said the sergeant. 'Have you ever seen her with one?'

'It's true Madison does make notes during our visits, but her notepad is quite small. That sheet of paper comes from an A5 pad and hers is half that size.'

'Have you seen anyone else making notes?'

'Several of the Austen enthusiasts do, especially the book club members.'

'Can you give us their names?'

'Kathleen Trueman occasionally jots things down, but usually on the itinerary booklet. The person who takes the most notes is Imogene Carnegie. She's passionate about Jane Austen, but I really couldn't tell you what size notebook she uses. I didn't pay that much attention.'

'Do you think she might have a grudge against you as well as Eshe Barbier?'

She licked her lips. 'There was an ugly scene at the theatre yesterday afternoon. Imogene accused me of victimising Madison and trying to break up their friendship. If her brother hadn't intervened, I thought she was going to physically attack me. She is a neurotic young woman and her brother said she is on medication for her nerves.'

'Interesting. But why would she use the exact same words in her note that you overheard Madison using?'

'A good point, Detective Sergeant. The only explanation I can come up with is that on Monday morning, after I'd made the position clear to Madison and she was still bristling at having to apologise to Madame Barbier, she had breakfast with the Carnegies and I noticed Imogene throwing me poisonous glances throughout the meal.'

'You believe Madison could have repeated those phrases in that conversation and Imogene picked up on them.'

Fiona sighed. 'It's possible, I suppose.'

'Of course, these notes may indicate someone has a grudge, but as no harm has come to you, there is nothing to suggest that they are death threats.'

'True.' Fiona managed a smile. At least she had a reason to feel a little less guilty for bringing up Imogene's name.

DI Swift snatched up the evidence sleeve, threw it into his briefcase and banged it shut. 'When you two have finished your little chat, can we get back to the matter in hand. Who had a motive for murdering Eshe Barbier?'

'It's difficult to see why any of her fellow travellers would go to such lengths. After all, none of the others have any association with her or Kinyande,' DS Sanders pointed out.

'Which means that Mosi remains our chief suspect? We're wasting our time here. That will be all, Mrs Mason, and I need a coffee.'

'I'll get it for you, Guv.' The DS jumped to his feet and hurried to the door in time to open it for Fiona.'

They walked the length of the corridor side by side. Fiona was still seething and as they were about to enter the lobby, she suddenly stopped.

'Is your boss for real?'

He raised an eyebrow.

'Does he usually act like some clichéd character in a badly written TV cop drama?'

His face contorted in the effort of trying not to laugh, but he could not prevent the grin.

'Not as a rule. To be fair, he's usually pretty laid back at interviews. But this is a major case. We don't get many murders on our patch and certainly never one quite as high-powered as this. He thought he had it all sewn up. A real feather in his cap to end his career and now it looks as if it's all falling apart.'

'So he decided to take it out on me.'

'Humph.' He shook his head. 'You're not the only one, believe me.'

She gave him a sympathetic grin. 'I've just had a thought. You said earlier that none of my other passengers had any previous knowledge of Madame Barbier or her country, but I'm not sure that's true. It's probably not relevant anyway, but I know one of the passengers was born in an ex-French colony somewhere in Africa. I don't know if it was in Kinyande.'

She told him about Renée.

'When we were having lunch before we went to Chawton house, Renée was asking Mosi where he was from. She mentioned Kinyande, to be exact, the country where the president was assassinated last month. I thought it strange that she seemed so persistent at the time. Of course, even if it was, it doesn't mean she came in contact with Madame Barbier or her husband.'

'True, but it's definitely something to follow up.'

He glanced at his watch. 'I better go. The governor's waiting for his coffee.'

Chapter 26

Back upstairs in her room, Fiona sat on the edge of her bed feeling utterly drained. It was all too clear that Mosi still remained at the top of the police list of suspects but at least DS Sanders had listened to her ideas. Whether he was trying to make up for his boss's aggressive attitude or he genuinely wasn't as obdurate as she had originally thought him, was impossible to tell. She still felt guilty telling him about Madame Barbier's spats with Madison and Imogene and even more so about Renée. As Winston would no doubt tell her, whatever she felt about their innocence, it would have been wrong not to mention it. Right now, there was absolutely nothing she could do about the situation so there was no point in agonising over it.

At breakfast, Winston had suggested that after her interview she should take the opportunity to relax and see more of what Bath had to offer by herself. It was true there was little chance of her leading another Footsteps Tour to the area, but sightseeing had never been on her agenda even before things started going wrong. There was no better time for her to fill in some of the paperwork. This was much the shortest tour she had ever led, but it had been so full on that apart from a few scrappy notes, not a single form was complete.

With a sigh, she pushed herself to her feet and went in search of the forms. The only plus was that on this tour she didn't need to bother with the reams of stuff required at the ferry ports and no passport details to worry about.

It was hard to motivate herself, but she eventually got into the swing of things and by half-past ten decided she had earned herself a coffee break.

She filled the kettle and was about to switch it on when

she decided against it. The little pots of UHT milk that the hotel provided in their rooms were always second best. Instead she would go down to the lounge and treat herself to a decent coffee, perhaps even a cake if they had anything that looked tempting. She could do with a sugar rush.

She was surprised to see so many of her party already gathered in the lounge. They were huddled in one corner talking excitedly. There was a considerable amount of headshaking.

Fiona bought herself a cappuccino at the coffee bar and walked over to them.

'Has something happened?'

Several people looked up sheepishly like naughty children caught doing something they shouldn't.

'You missed a real bit of excitement,' said Erma who clearly had no such scruples. 'The police have arrested Imogene.'

'We don't know that,' snapped Kathleen.

'I was having my interview with the sergeant when this dreadful hysterical screaming broke out in the next room. It was so bad, that he had to go and see what was happening,' said Erma. 'He'd left the door slightly open and a minute or so later I saw him rush back down the corridor. He must have gone to fetch Piers because they both came back and went in next door. Things calmed down a bit then and the sergeant came back in. I think he must have forgotten all about me because he seemed surprised to see me still sitting there. Naturally, I asked him what had happened. He wouldn't answer me, just said I could go.'

'But what makes you think Imogene has been arrested?'

'I went to the ladies and when I was coming back here, I saw them all in the lobby. Imogene was still crying. Piers had his arm round her shoulder, and I heard her telling him she was sorry and something about not meaning to do it. Then the inspector and another policeman took them both off in a car.'

'But as I keep telling you,' said Franklin, 'if she'd been arrested for killing Estelle, why are the police continuing to conduct interviews? Renée's in there with the DS right now. She's been in there for almost half an hour. Heaven knows why. I was in and out with the inspector in five minutes.'

'It's a bit of the luck of the draw, I think. Anthony and I were the same. DS Sanders seems to take far longer than the inspector.'

'Except for Madison. She was first in and her interview took ages,' said Ruth. 'Perhaps the police thought she was an obvious suspect. We all saw her pick that fight with Estelle on the first evening.'

'Maybe, but you can't have it both ways. If as you claim, the police have arrested Imogene, then Madison can no longer be a suspect for Estelle's murder.'

'Well whoever did it, good luck to them. She was a perfectly odious woman and if you ask me, the world's a better place without her.'

'Erma! That's a wicked thing to say,' admonished Kathleen.

Erma shrugged, not in the least chastened.

'Does anyone know where Madison is now?' asked Fiona trying to sooth the tension.

'She went straight out once her interview was over,' said Erma. 'Said something about going to the Royal Crescent to find that Georgian House the guide mentioned on the walking tour, but it wouldn't surprise me if she's disappeared for good.'

Time to intervene and try and change the subject.

'Didn't you two want to go and see the sights as well?' Fiona asked Kathleen.

Erma got to her feet clearly in a huff at being ignored. 'I think I'll go for a walk in the grounds.'

Kathleen frowned. 'I do apologise on Erma's behalf, Fiona. I really don't know what's got into her these last few days. She's never been this abrasive before.'

'It's hardly your fault.'

'No, but I do feel responsible. Anyway, to answer your question, we did think about going to see the Roman Baths. Anthony's feeling a bit tired this morning and even though we'd planned to order a taxi, after all that's happened, neither of us were in the mood really. These interviews have put a real dampener on the holiday.' Kathleen gave a heartfelt sigh. 'If you'll all forgive me, I've still got a little packing to do.'

Fiona sat back drinking her coffee for a few minutes before turning to Franklin, 'What sort of things did the inspector want to know?'

'Once he'd asked me who was still in the tapestry room when I left, he only had a couple more questions. Not that I could tell him much, anyway. I wasn't paying that much attention. Don't have a clue who was where when.'

'He didn't ask you if you had any connections with Kinyande?'

Franklin looked surprised. 'He did actually. Is that what he asked you?'

She shook her head. 'Kinyande is where your wife was born, isn't it?'

He looked at Fiona in surprise. 'Yes, but I've never been there.'

'I've never heard of it. Where is it?' asked Ruth, the only other person now left in the lounge.

'It's in Central Africa.'

'Is that where Estelle came from?'

Fiona nodded. 'She was the wife of the president who was assassinated about three weeks ago.'

'Really?' Franklin stared at her wide eyed.

'But his name wasn't du Plessis,' he protested.

'No. Du Plessis wasn't Estelle's real name either.' With her eyes still locked on his, Fiona continued, 'Did Renée recognise her?'

Franklin's jaw dropped. After a long silence, he stammered, 'If she did, she didn't tell me.'

186

Chapter 27

Franklin had left soon after Fiona had dropped her bombshell. It hadn't had quite the effect that she had expected, but it had produced a reaction. She was certain of that. If only she could work out what had been out of tune. Something hadn't been quite right, but what? There was so little time left. In less than three hours everyone would be leaving and the chances of catching the killer might well be lost.

She wondered if DS Sanders was still interviewing Renée. It wouldn't hurt to go and see. She walked out into the lobby to see June and Lester Summerhayes on their way out.

'I know it's a bit late in the day, but we've decided to visit the Roman Baths. Seems silly not to see them when we've come all this way. We have a taxi waiting for us to save a bit of time. We'll try to get back for lunch, but if we are a little late, you'll know where we are.'

Fiona smiled. 'No problem. At least the grey skies have disappeared, and the sun's now shining.'

She walked slowly along the corridor, the door to the room where she had been interviewed by the inspector was now open and the room empty. She could hear a low voice coming from the next room. Perhaps the interview was still in progress. The door was slightly ajar enough for her to see someone standing at the window with his back to her. DS Sanders held a police radio to his ear. She was about to make a tactful withdrawal when he suddenly snapped it off.

'Bloody man!'

The vehemence in his voice made her jump. He must have noticed the movement because he looked up.

'Sorry about that, come in.'

Wearily he pulled the chair from under the table and sank

down.

'What can I do for you, Mrs Mason?'

'I didn't mean to disturb you. I just wondered if the interviews were over.'

He nodded. 'All done. The inspector's just left.'

'There's a rumour going around that Imogene Carnegie has been arrested.'

'Good heavens, no. Whatever made people think that?'

'One of my people saw her and her brother being driven off in a police car.'

'To the hospital not the station. She's had some sort of breakdown. According to her brother, their doctor prescribed anti-depressants but it's clear the woman is unstable. I'm not saying she's certifiable, but she does need help.'

'Was she responsible for the poison pen letters?'

'She denied it at first, but we found the notebook the sheets were torn from in her room. That's when she went to pieces.'

'Poor woman.'

'It's her brother I feel sorry for. But then he's not exactly your normal type either.'

'So, if no one has been arrested for Madame Barbier's murder, what now?'

'I wish I knew. We've uncovered a few skeletons as well as obvious reasons why several people had a possible cause to want to take revenge on the woman. What we haven't got is anything that adds up to a solid motive for a carefully planned and executed murder.'

'Does that mean everyone is free to go?'

'I've got nothing to hold them on.'

He leant forward putting his elbows on the table, rubbing his face.

Not certain if this was her cue to leave, she got to her feet. His head snapped up; his eyes locked on hers.

'Don't go. I need your help.'

She sank back down. The surprise must have shown on

her face because he said, 'As things stand right now, as far as anyone outside is concerned, this is just another case involving the murder of a foreign tourist, but once it gets out that our Estelle du Plessis was a high profile figure, the bigwigs from the National Murder Squad will sweep in and take over.'

Dare she admit that the cat was already out of the bag and she was the one who had set it free by announcing it to the other passengers, no matter that was in the hope that it would provoke a reaction. In the general scheme of things, word would get out and it would be all over the media.

He sighed and rubbed a hand over his face again.

'If I don't make an arrest, it could scupper any chance of promotion.'

'But isn't Detective Inspector Swift in charge of the case?'

He pulled a face.

'You mean if the case is successful, the inspector gets the glory but if no one is arrested, you will get the blame.'

'Something like that. It's the same the world over.' He sighed. 'I got it in the neck for not taking Mosi Timbili into custody when I first interviewed him on Monday evening. At the time, we had no idea Eshe Barbier's death was anything other than natural causes. I'm convinced her murderer is one of your party but, with nothing to hold them, I can't see that I have any choice but to let them all go.'

After a long silence, she said, 'You spent a long time interviewing certain people.'

'It didn't get us anywhere. I'm being honest with you, Mrs Mason, this is against my better judgement but according to Peter Montgomery-Jones, I should trust your judgement. He also said you were discreet.'

Ouch. If only he knew.

'I'm asking for your help.'

'I'm not sure I can.'

'You know these people far better than I. Is there anything, anything at all, that has happened that strikes you as odd looking back?'

189

She hesitated. 'I take it you are aware that Renée Austin was born in Kinyande. I don't know the circumstances, but I believe her sister died out there.'

He nodded. 'She died of cancer in a hospital.'

'Is that what Renée told you?'

'Yes, but we have confirmed it.'

'That scotches that idea.'

'I think any bitterness Mrs Austin might harbour is directed specifically at the militia who forced her sister and brother-in-law off their farm some years earlier. She did admit that her sister's health took a downward spiral from that point on.'

'The reason I mentioned it is because I think there's a good chance that Renée recognised Madame Barbier. I think she may have challenged her and that was the cause of the argument between them.'

'She made no mention of recognising Eshe Barbier.' He scratched his chin thoughtfully, then shook his head. 'Though even if she did, as far as we could discern, Mrs Austin has no cause to blame her specifically. Her sister's death occurred two years before Barbier's One Nation Party came to power. Mrs Austin admitted that she and Madame Barbier exchanged heated words but that was because she took exception to the woman's rudeness when she ridiculed Renée's lack of knowledge about Jane Austen's work.'

'That was typical of Madame Barbier, I'm afraid.'

'We are well aware that in the short time she was a member of the tour party, she upset several others which resulted in some very public arguments, never mind those she offended. Though we have investigated exactly what took place on each occasion, there does not appear to be anything that might result in anyone having a credible cause for planning and executing the murder.'

'Which I presume means that Mosi still remains at the top of your suspect list.'

He pulled a face then sighed. 'Not specially. Even if I don't buy his explanation for following her over to this country or the fact that this chap back in Kinyande, Faucher or whatever his name is, vouches for Timbili, insisting the man came here at his request, I have a problem with how she was killed.'

'Oh?'

'As your Mr Peter Montgomery-Jones made very clear,' he said with a touch of bitterness in his voice, 'there were so many much easier ways to get rid of her that would have diverted suspicion. Timbili's best opportunity was when he first arrived in the hotel in Winchester and went to her room. Which he admits was one of the first things he did, though not to kill her but to plead for her return to Kinyande. If his purpose was murder, he could have given her an overdose at that point. Even if he knew an overdose would not be instant, he could have stayed to ensure that she did not summon help. When her body was found, there would be no reason to suspect foul play and her death put down to her accidently giving herself an overdose when her usual routine was upset by her travelling to Winchester.'

'What happens now?'

'Assuming there is nothing more you can tell me, I'll go through all the statements and all the background info the team have managed to collate once more and see if there is anything I've missed.'

'In which case, I'll leave you to it.'

As she reached the door, he called after her. 'I may not have identified the murderer, but I am one hundred per cent certain, he or she is one of your party, Mrs Mason.'

'So am I, Detective Sergeant. That is what is worrying me as much as it is you.'

Chapter 28

On the plus side, it looked as though Mosi was no more a suspect than any of the others, but Fiona was as reluctant to see the killer go free, which they almost certainly would be once lunch was over and everyone was homeward bound.

The nagging feeling that she had missed a vital clue was back. There was something she'd seen or heard she could not quite recall hovering on the edge of her memory. Perhaps some fresh air would help.

There was a set of shallow steps on the patio outside the restaurant which led down to the broad grassed terrace. She sat down on the top step, lifted her face to the sun and closed her eyes. Taking long gentle breaths, she let her mind go blank. The only sounds were the splashing of water in the fountain in the centre of the formal garden to her left and the occasional distant call of a blackbird in the trees beyond.

Suddenly it came to her. She jumped up and almost ran to where she had left DS Sanders.

'Forgive me barging in again, but I've been thinking…'

~

Montgomery-Jones decided to stop off at his flat for a quick shower and a change of clothes before going into the office. He unlocked the front door and without stopping to remove his coat, walked straight through to his study, placed his briefcase onto the desk and picked up the receiver.

'Good morning, James. I have just returned. I should be back in the office in half an hour. Have there been any developments I do not know about since I left?'

'I was about to ring you, sir. There was a call from Jean-Claude Durand an hour ago to say he's managed to arrange

192

for our trade delegate to join the French nationals and the plane will be arriving first thing tomorrow. I've arranged for him to be met by our man out there and taken to Rabat airport. I've booked him a seat on a standard flight back to Heathrow.'

'That is good news. I will inform the Foreign Secretary straight away.'

'Already done, sir. And I've left a message for the Minister for Trade and Industry at his office.'

'Good work, James. Is there anything that requires my immediate attention?'

'No, sir.'

'In which case, I will see you later.'

He replaced the receiver and pushed himself to his feet stifling a yawn. There was no reason not to get his head down for the next hour or so.

~

It was in their hands now. There was nothing more she could do.

The sun was still shining but a cool breeze had sprung up. Nothing to stop her walking down the gravel path through the clump of mature trees towards the little humpback bridge over the stream that ran through the property to the park beyond.

Someone else obviously had the same idea. As she came out of the trees, she saw Erma standing in the centre of the stone bridge with her back to her looking down into the water below.

'Ruth not with you? Sorry, I didn't mean to make you jump.'

'I didn't hear you coming. She's gone back up to her room to do some last-minute packing.'

Erma didn't look best pleased at Fiona's arrival.

'You looked lost in thought there.'

'I was just wondering if the coach will be leaving straight

after lunch as planned. Have you been told?'

'Not specifically, but Winston had all the big cases loaded and everything is set to go.'

'That's good.'

'I expect it all depends on whether or not Estelle's murderer has been identified.'

'But the police can't prevent us from leaving, can they?'

'I really couldn't say.'

'They have to have a good reason for detaining us.'

'Perhaps they have. After all, Estelle was murdered inside Chawton House, so her killer had to be one of our party.'

'But that's ridiculous. The stupid woman could have given herself an overdose. It probably wasn't murder at all.'

'How did you know she died of an overdose?'

Erma turned her head and stared directly at her, opening and closing her mouth, then just as quickly turned back to face the stream, both hands on the capping stones along the bridge wall. 'That's what everyone was saying,' she muttered.

'Really? That's news to me.'

Fiona let the silence hang for a good minute. 'I believe that floppy velvet bag of hers is being tested for fingerprints.'

Erma's hands visibly tighten their grip. 'I picked it up for her when she left it in the garden at the museum.'

'I expect that was when you remembered she carried her medication in it. Is that when you stole the injector pen and spare phial? Or was it later when you saw her in the garden at Chawton House?'

'I don't know what you're talking about?'

'It must have been a shock when you saw her arrive for the house tour. You expected her to collapse in the garden then and there, didn't you? You must have been desperate to get her on her own again. Too risky to try stabbing her a second time in full view of the rest of us. What luck for you that she stayed behind in the tapestry room. What happened then? Did she collapse on that tiny flight of stairs leading up to the offices?' Erma's eyes widened and her face was

194

suddenly pale.

Fiona knew she'd hit the mark. 'The last thing you needed was for someone to see her and summon help. Is that when you decided to roll her body onto the landing and pull that small screen in front. Though just to make sure, you reloaded the pen from the extra phial and jabbed her a second time.'

'Why on earth would I, of all people, want to kill Estelle du Plessis? I'd never ever met the woman until last Sunday.'

'You may not have done, but your beloved big sister certainly did. She knew Estelle – let's call her by her real name Eshe – extremely well. She was her governess, wasn't she? What happened to your sister? What did Eshe Barbier do to her that she had to die?'

The older woman's normally pleasant, rounded face twisted into an unpleasant sneer and before Fiona had a chance to defend herself, she felt the full force of a heavy leather shoulder bag slam against her left temple, knocking her sideways. With an agility surprising for a woman in her late sixties, Erma hopped over Fiona's now recumbent body half-collapsed against the upstream wall of the bridge and began racing up the gravel path towards the hotel. Fiona pushed herself to her feet and turned just in time to see Erma run straight into the arms of Detective Sergeant Sanders.

Her head was still spinning so she stood and watched as a uniformed policeman handcuffed the struggling woman hurling abuse at both officers. She heard him give Erma the customary caution before leading her away.

DS Sanders looked back at Fiona. 'Are you okay, Mrs Mason?'

Fiona waved a hand. 'I'll be fine. You go on. I'll join you when I've got my breath back.'

She took her time slowly walking up the path.

Chapter 29

DS Sanders came to tell her he was leaving.

'I can't thank you enough. I very much doubt we'd have cracked this case without you. As you suggested, we looked into Erma Mahoney née Pettigrew's family details and we discovered she had an older sister. The sister died in a prison in Kindessi. A bit of a hellhole so I understand. She'd been accused of theft. What I don't understand is how you worked it all out.'

'I had no idea about how her sister died or why Erma blamed Madame Barbier for it. All I do know is that when we were all sitting outside the pub where we'd stopped for coffee, Erma reacted rather oddly when Estelle, as we knew her then, was talking about her love of Jane Austen being fostered by her governess, a Miss Pettigrew who used to read her Jane's novels at bedtime. Later that day, Erma mentioned that her sister had been a governess. Going over everything in my mind this morning, I just wondered if the two things were connected.'

'Which we discovered they were.'

'Have you any idea why Erma blamed Madame Barbier for her sister's death?'

'It's not in any records but according to Mrs Mahoney herself, Eshe was given an expensive piece of jewellery, a diamond necklace by her father for her fifteenth birthday. One evening on a night out, Eshe wanted to wear it to impress her friends and took it from the safe in her father's study without telling him. Eshe lost the necklace and knowing she would be severely punished, she claimed that she had seen Miss Pettigrew steal it. Whether the story is true or not I've no idea, but that's what Erma believes.'

'Was I right about how she killed Madame Barbier?'

'Almost, although she claims she did it on impulse. She saw Madame Barbier alone in the garden at Chawton House, she was bent down photographing some flowers. Erma saw the bag lying a few feet away. She picked it up intending to return it but, if you believe her story, before she realised what she was doing, she'd slipped her hand inside, grabbed the epi-pen and stuck it into Estelle's shoulder. When Madame Barbier turned up for the house tour, she was worried she be accused of attempted murder. Later, when Madame Barbier left her bag on one of the dining chairs, Erma waited until no one was looking and took the bag, extracted the spare phial then hid the bag behind the curtain.'

Fiona shook her head. 'Erma could be abrasive and bad-tempered, but I never pictured her as a murderer.'

'Strange woman. And certainly not repentant. In fact, she seemed quite proud of herself. More than happy to tell us exactly how she did it.'

'So much for all the political angle. A simple case of revenge and retribution.'

'My car's waiting. I'll be off. You and your party are now free to enjoy your final lunch together.'

She walked with him to the door of the hotel.

He shook her hand and said, 'I'm very grateful for your help, Mrs Mason, but once you'd told us your suspicions and put us on the right path, you really should have left it in our hands and not tried to tackle the woman yourself. She is so ruthless; I doubt she'd have any qualms about killing you. How's the head, by the way?'

'I'm fine, thank you. Though I admit at the time, it did feel like she had a brick in her bag when she swung it at me like that. And as for tackling her, believe me, Sergeant, nothing was further from my mind. I went for a breath of fresh air and just happened to come across her. I had no idea she'd be there.'

'Maybe, but it didn't stop you challenging her, did it?'
'Umm.'

'You were lucky she didn't injure you more seriously. She could have killed you, the state she was in.'

'I admit I was lucky you came when you did.' Best to keep him sweet even if Erma had taken to her heels before he came into view.

'We went to her room to arrest her, but her roommate said she was still in the garden which is why we came looking.'

'I think your driver is waiting.'

She turned to go back into the hotel and almost bumped into someone standing behind her.

'Was that DS Sanders?'

'Madison! I'm sorry I didn't see you there. Yes, it was. Are you okay?'

Fiona was shocked to see how pale and haggard the girl looked.

Madison brushed a bedraggled lock of hair from her face and wearily shifted her rucksack strap to her other shoulder.

'I came back the other way. What about the inspector; is he still here?' She peered suspiciously through the open front door.

'No. He left over an hour ago. All the police are gone.'

'Thank goodness for small mercies. Does that mean we have to wait around till they find more evidence?'

'No. The case is over. We can all relax and enjoy our final lunch together before we all make our separate ways back home.'

'I don't understand. What do you mean, it's over? Have they arrested someone?'

'Oh yes.' Fiona put a hand on Madison's arm and gently guided her inside. 'I don't suppose there's any harm in you knowing. It will be all over the media by tonight.'

By the time she had answered all of Madison's questions they had climbed the stairs up to the third floor. They arrived at the door to Fiona's room and Madison made to go on, but Fiona called her back.

'Just a moment. I have something to give you. Come on in.'

Madison looked apprehensive as Fiona picked up the gift from the shelf below the television and held it out.

'It won't bite! Take it.'

'Is this my report?'

Fiona laughed. 'In a paper bag! Hardly. It's just a small token to say thank you for all your help. I bought it for you at the Jane Austen Centre, but I haven't had time to wrap it properly. Things have been hectic since then to say the least.'

Tentatively, Madison opened the paper bag and drew out the book. Suddenly, her eyes were full of tears and she sank down onto the edge of the bed and began to sob noisily.

'What on earth's the matter?'

Fiona seized a handful of tissues from the box on the shelf and stuffed them into the girl's hand before sitting down beside her, her arm around her shoulder.

It took a minute for the girl to answer. 'I thought you were going to give me a copy of your report on me. I've been dreading it all morning. After all the other crap that's happened today, I thought it would be the last straw.'

'Did the inspector give you a hard time?'

'Not specially. He tried to make out I had a motive at first, but I told him there were plenty of other people who Estelle had crossed swords with, but...' Her face went red and she ground to a halt.

'Go on.'

'As I went out, I heard him talking to the constable in there with him. He called me... He called me a vengeful, empty-headed kid with grandiose ideas of my own importance. Totally unreliable as a witness.'

When Fiona made no comment, she slid her a quick sidelong look before continuing. 'I was pretty upset so I went to the lounge to find Imogene. Piers said she'd just popped back to the room to fetch a cardigan, so I told him what the inspector had said.'

'What was his reaction?'

Madison's bottom lip quivered. 'Let's just say, he wasn't very sympathetic. Then the others started laying into me. Even Kathleen said the childish game I had played with Imogene choosing similar costumes for the ball was beneath me and she hoped I'd be grown-up enough to give you an apology before I left.'

Madison picked up the book running her fingers over the flowers on the cover. 'It's beautiful. I don't deserve this. I've been sitting in the park all morning going over everything. I've been a right pain-in-the-arse. I realise that now. I'm sorry.'

'I can't deny there have been times when you've been more of a hindrance than a help, but let's put all that behind us and just say, you still have a lot to learn. But right now, I think we both better get on or we'll be late for lunch.' She looked at her watch. 'I've a couple of important phone calls I need to make and change back into my uniform.'

'Okay.' Madison paused at the door and looked back over her shoulder. 'And thanks again, Fiona. I don't think I could ever do your job. Heaven knows why I thought I could.'

Once the girl had gone, Fiona took her mobile from her pocket. David Rushworth would be relieved to know that everything was over.

Her second call was answered after two rings.

'Peter. I thought you might like to know…'

She carefully avoided telling him about her part in bringing Madame Barbier's murderer to justice and her confrontation with Erma on the bridge, concentrating only on the unrepentant woman's arrest and confession to DS Sanders.

'That is good news. I take it you have not yet informed Mosi Timbili?'

'Not yet. The police have only just left the hotel.'

'Would you like me to come and collect you?'

'Certainly not. It's time you went home to catch up on some sleep. You must have been up most of the night with everything that's been going on. Besides, it's best if I travel back with Winston and the book club people after lunch. I can't stop the story getting out, but I do need to stop any wild rumours spreading among the passengers. Plus, I have to try to protect Super Sun Executive Travel's reputation as the country's top company for quality coach tours.'

'If you are certain.'

'Absolutely. Although…'

'Yes?'

It was now or never. 'If you don't mind picking me up from Victoria Coach Station when we get back to London, and assuming you are not busy for the rest of the weekend, I could stay for a few days before returning home. We should be there around four o'clock.'

There was a chuckle at the end of the line. 'Excellent idea. I will be waiting.'

ACKNOWLEDGMENTS

My special thanks to Clio O'Sullivan at Chawton House Library for all her help during lockdown.

As always thanks to my wonderful beta readers and all who have helped me. The list is too long to name individually but be assured I value each and every one of you.

A note from the author

Thank you for reading. I hope you enjoyed the book as much as I enjoyed writing it. It seems impossible these days to buy anything online, visit a restaurant or any kind of attraction without being asked to write a review. Even service industries request feedback. I appreciate just how annoying that can be, but Indie writers like me are totally dependent upon reviews. Thousands of new books are published on a weekly basis and every review for *Blood Follows Jane Austen* on Amazon helps push it higher up the charts and so make it more visible to potential new readers. I would be so grateful if you would consider spending a few minutes writing an honest review for me. It need only be a sentence or two to say why you liked the book.

www.judithcranswick.co.uk

Printed in Great Britain
by Amazon